seeing green

Book 3

Pine Hills Series
Book Three

laramie cummings

I0835626

copyright

The characters and events portrayed in this book are fictitious. Any similarity to real persons, living or dead, is coincidental and not intended by the author.

Ebook ISBN: 978-1-967594-08-5

ISBN: 978-1-967594-09-2, 978-1-967594-06-1

First Publication: 2026

Cover design by: Get Covers, getcovers.com

Publisher: WYde Open Pages , owner@wydeopenpages.com

www.llcummingsbooks.com

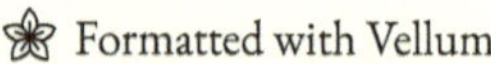

For all the women who have carried a grief to heavy. You are not alone.

a note to my readers

content warning

Your well-being and mental health are important to me. This story touches on some themes that may be difficult for some readers. If the topics below are something you feel challenging, please take care of yourself as you decide whether to continue. It's okay to step away or skip parts of the story if you need to. Your comfort and peace come first.

Content Warnings:

- Miscarriage - Discussion about Medical Abortion - Depictions of grief and loss - Alcohol consumption - Use of profanity

soundtrack

To listen to the Seeing Green soundtrack click the link or scan the QR code. Happy listening.

Apple Music: Seeing Green Spotify: Seeing Green

Apple Music Playlist

Soundtrack

Spotify Playlist

prologue

emma

10 YEARS OLD...

There is nothing like seeing Jonathan Taylor Thomas in my *Teen Beat* magazine. He is the absolute definition of everything I want in a man with his tan skin, blue eyes, and light brown hair. I am thoroughly obsessed, and I just know that one day we will be together. He is—or at least will be mine, eventually. But for now, I will continue to just stare into those ocean eyes that are on page 21 of *Teen Beat* and think of my future when I can stare into them for real.

"Emmmmmmmm!!!!!"

I bolt up in my bed so fast, frantically trying to hide my obsession under my blanket as my older brother, Everett, barges into my room. I see that he has a friend over, and I feel mortified that my brother walked in without even a single knock.

"Emma. What's up, chicken butt? Want to come hang out by the pool with Joel and me?"

"First off, knock next time. And second, who is Joel?"

"My new best friend." Everett looked at me with the look only siblings can decipher. The look that said I needed to play it cool or I would feel his wrath later.

"Uh, okay," I said.

Joel stepped around Everett, and at first, I couldn't quite tell what he looked like. Was he cute? Not cute? But once I got a good look at him, I saw that he had light brown hair and tanned skin just like JTT. My heart fluttered like a hummingbird, but it was probably just still acting that way because of my reaction to *Teen Beat's* article on JTT.

"This is Joel. He and his parents are visiting here for a few weeks at a lake house. They know Mom and Dad, and thought we could hang out with him while he is here. So pool?"

"Sure. Why not?"

Scooting off my bed, Joel finally looked up at me. Standing in front of him and seeing what he looked like, I swooned. He was a few inches taller than me, with tan skin, green eyes, and brown hair. This boy was better than Jonathan. This boy was my new everything. Joel was going to be my husband someday. I knew it and felt it down to my bones (or whatever adults said).

"H-h-hi. I'm Joel."

"Yes, I will," I replied.

"Will what?" He asked, sounding confused.

"Oh, nothing. I was just saying I will go swimming. See you two down there. Get out so I can change." I turned towards my brother and pushed him out of my room.

"Cool. Can you bring some Capri's? Or Kool-aid?" Everett asked.

"Yes. Now get out!"

The boys left, and I slammed my door shut. I slumped against my door and felt my heart beat right out of my chest. I swore I could see it thumping if I looked down. It was faster than the bus in the movie *Speed.* I needed it to slow down before I went out in a swimsuit to see my new love and eventual husband.

In my entire ten years of life, I never thought I would fall for another boy other than JTT. But today changed my life trajectory. From here on out, I would do everything to make sure that Joel was or would be mine. Before that, I needed to get into my favorite suit and look cute. I immediately put on my red polka dot bikini, applied a generous swipe of Juice Smackers lip balm, brushed my hair until it looked like Marsha's from The Brady Bunch, and performed a very critical inspection of myself in the mirror. This better make his "jaw drop," as my mother liked to say when she put on fancy dresses, because I looked freaking good.

Fifteen minutes later, I was sitting on the edge of the pool watching Joel and Everett throw a football back and forth, back and forth, back and forth. Joel hadn't looked at me even once. Was I not cute enough for him? I thought that by wearing my cutest bikini, he would have at least looked at me, but he just kept looking down or away from me. Maybe he didn't really like me. What if my brother told him something embarrassing, and so he really didn't like me or want to play with me? I vowed right then and there to get to the bottom of it.

"Want to play Marco Polo?" I asked.

"Yeah! Let's play. I will be first." Everett said. He loved being first at everything.

"Cool," was all Joel said.

"Alright, the rules are that you have to stay in the water at all times. You can't get out. I am going to close my eyes and start counting to twenty-five so you can get a good spot. Ready? One...two..."

Joel moved to the shallow end corner. Hopping in, I glided over to him. He finally looked at me, and his eyes went wide. They were this really rich green, and I swear I would have fainted like the ladies in the old movies if I weren't in water.

"I'm just standing here until he comes over," I whispered.

"Uh, okay." He whispered back a little rudely.

This situation was not going well.

I was getting mad.

"No need to be a jerk," I whispered.

"Sorry. I'm shy." He whispered.

"Well, if you're my brother's new best friend, you'd better learn how to talk to me. Besides, we are going to get married someday as long as you stop being a meanie. I whispered, yelled.

"Twenty...twenty-one..."

"Really?" He whispered back.

"Yup."

"Cool."

We stared at each other, and in the space between our silence, it was like a million conversations took place between us. At that moment, my eyes locked onto Joel's deep green eyes. It made me forget all about Jonathan Taylor Thomas's blue ones.

"MARCO!" yelled Everett.

"POLO!" We both yelled back, still staring into each other's eyes.

1
emma

SUMMER, *9 years later...*

Today was the day of my summer break when I, Emma Elizabeth Manning, was going to ask Joel Christopher Clarence out to the Pine Hills Summer dance. I pep-talked myself in the mirror as I tried on shirt after shirt, making sure that I looked hot. "Work It" by Missy Elliott was playing in the background to pump me up. I was going to ask him as soon as he got here to pregame with Ev and Lane. I settled on my cute black Victoria's Secret string bikini, followed by my Abercrombie navy shirt and jean shorts, double-checked my hair and makeup, and made sure my Tiffany's heart necklace was lying perfectly on my neck. Feeling satisfied, I left and joined my brother in his red Jeep Wrangler to head to the lake.

"Are you going to do it?" Piper asked me after we got to the lake and were setting up our spot. Piper was friends with Lane and my brother, so she became one of mine. She was older, but we clicked. She knew about my crazy crush on Joel and always tried to help me get a leg up on sitting next to him, being his partner, or whatever I needed to be close to him.

"Yes. Right before the beach volleyball starts, I am going to do it before any of the other girls get here. It should give me time to execute my plan. Do I look good?" I asked, twirling in front of her, wearing only my bikini.

"Girl, you always look hot. Have you been doing squats in college? Because I am jealous of that bootay. Now go and get 'em."

"Thanks! I have been. I appreciate you complimenting me on my hard work." My confidence level skyrocketed to a solid ten after she told me it looked good. I had been working out and was elated about the noticeable results.

The butterflies started in my stomach. I was asking Joel to the town's summer dance, and I only had about three seconds to breathe before I plopped down on the sand next to him.

"Hey, Em."

"Hiya!"

"How was your morning?"

"Great."

I froze, and he just stared.

"Are you okay?" Joel asked with a quizzical tilt to his voice.

"Yuh, yes. Um. No. Well, I have something to ask you."

"Oh. Well, shoot."

"Um..." I turned in my stool to look him dead on, "Do you by chance have a date to the dance?"

"No, I don't." His cheeks started to flush. My mind wandered, wondering if my cheeks were bright red, too. Oh God, this was so embarrassing and nerve-wracking.

"Oh. Um ... bummer." I looked away from him out at the sparkling lake. The sun was reflecting off the surface perfectly, casting a million dancing lights.

"Emma?"

"Yeah?"

"Was that all you wanted to ask me?" Again, he was quizzical.

"No. It wasn't." I stared at my painted pink toes in the sand.

"So, you gonna tell me what you wanted to ask?"

"I guess." I took a deep breath and, still staring at my toes buried deep in the sand, asked, "Would you go with me?"

"Can you look at me?"

Suddenly, two large, warm hands grasped my face, turning me to look directly towards Joel. He was looking directly at me. Joel's lean but muscular torso turned, and he had his hands still on my face. His thumbs started to rub my cheeks.

"Can you ask me and look at me?" He had the tiniest bit of a smirk.

"Yes?" Another big breath, "Will you be my date?"

"Sure."

"Really?"

"Yup. It will be fun."

"Cool." My nerves dissipated, and I gazed longingly into his emerald eyes. They were striking. They were definitely a green field you could get lost in.

A loud clearing of the throat shattered the moment. I looked over, seeing Piper staring the two of us down. We both turned away to face the lake. I pretended through the rest of day that nothing happened and trying to suppress my goofy, blissed-out smile that wanted to keep taking over my face.

On Saturday, I woke up and got ready for the dance with Piper and other friends who were home from college for the summer. I had chosen a beautiful green two-piece halter dress that looked like the deepest green of Joel's eyes, with swirls of turquoise and lighter greens to match mine. It was sleek and flowing, with a provocative high slit on the skirt. The halter top helped to lift my boobs perfectly. I felt truly beautiful.

At five, all the boys, including my brother, came to the house to pick us up. The boys had all gotten ready at Joel's house. Everyone was excited to see each other and take photos. I was vibrating with a dangerous mix of excitement and nervousness because I was going to the dance with Joel. I kept my fingers crossed, hoping that we might kiss, end up dating, and then get married, but who was keeping track of what could happen?

When my mother called us downstairs, I knew I had to make this moment perfect. I had to gracefully walk down the staircase to the foyer and lock eyes with Joel. I needed to make sure his gaze was only on me and that I wowed the socks off him.

All of us girls stepped out, and I let them all go down first. Trailing behind and taking several steps down to the first landing, I finally looked down to see where Joel was. Joel's back was towards me. All I could see was that he was wearing loose linen pants, and a collared green button-up. His muscular frame was dominating, and I could tell he definitely worked out in college. I took a few more steps down to finish my descent, but he still didn't turn around. I took my final step down, and Joel still didn't turn around. He was too busy talking to Everett. Strolling up to him ferociously, I tapped him on his impressively massive shoulder. He finally turned his head my way.

"Oh, hey there, Em."

"You didn't even watch my *She's All That* moment. How rude." I accused, my voice laced with offense.

"What? What are you talking about?"

In front of everyone, I threw up my arms and pointed dramatically to the staircase, "I walked sexily down the stairs just like Laney Boggs, and I didn't even trip. And you didn't notice. You were too busy. Rude is what you are, Joel. Rude." I tried to play it off as if I was joking, even though I was a bit butthurt. I stomped over to the entry table in the foyer, grabbed the boutonniere I had gotten him from the tray on the foyer table, and ripped the box open. Marching up to him, I pinned the white rose to his shirt pocket and stabbed the pin hard through the material into his chest.

"Ow, Em!"

"Serves you right, asshole."

I spun on my cute green heels, taking in the rest of the people in the foyer. "Is it time for photos?"

2
emma

3 HOURS LATER...

I was ready to leave. The dance was cute, happening in the town square. The Pine Hills town square was decorated with lights, a removable wood dance floor, and even had a stage for the band. What absolutely sucked about the night was that Joel and I had only danced two dances together, and when we did, he held me at arm's length like I had a contagious disease. It was painfully platonic. My romantic bubble had been thoroughly popped. I was over the whole thing and ready to head back to our pool house for the after-party. My parents had said we could have friends over after the dance, as they would also be having friends over after the community summer fling. It was tradition for the after-party to happen at our house. Kids were always sequestered to the pool house while the parents roamed on the back deck and the main house.

Walking up to my brother and his band of friends, I yelled over the music, "I hate this. I am going to call Carla to pick me up for a ride home. See you in a bit."

My brother nodded,, and I left, grabbing my purse that hung from a chair near Joel. I walked out towards the street along the square and opened my flip phone to call our house manager, Carla. Just then, a large hand grasped my wrist.

"Whoa! Where do you think you're going, Em?"

It was Joel. And I was furious. Tonight sucked.

"Home. See you there soon."

I turned away and started walking down Main Street towards home. I needed to get away from him because I was so pissed.

He jogged after me.

"Emma, wait. I'm sorry." I felt his hand on my shoulder, and he turned me around to face him.

"You're sorry? Tonight blew. It was the worst date I have ever been on." Tears gathered at the edge of my eyes. I was so utterly frustrated because the boy I had been crushing on for nearly a decade was failing spectacularly to live up to my dreams.

"It did, and I'm so sorry. To clarify, I didn't realize it was a date. I thought you just wanted to go with me because you wanted a person to go with. Also, I got a bit into my head. Your brother ... well ... I just couldn't... and ... well, how about I head to your house with you? I can help you set up."

"I have no idea what you just said. Your explanation is a freaking mess, and I am so pissed."

"I am going to go with you. I will make it up to you, I promise."

I had no idea what was happening, but I trusted him. But I needed him to explain everything. I groaned.

"Fine. You can come home with me and help me make sure everything is set up. But you'd better find the words to explain yourself better."

"Deal." He said with a soft smile.

45 minutes later ...

Everything was set up and ready to go. The dance should be over in about an hour, and I was ready. Joel hadn't said much, and it just made everything really awkward. When I told him everything looked fine. We sat awkwardly and in silence on the couch in the pool house. Thankfully, I had both changed into more comfortable clothing, so I wouldn't have to add physical discomfort to my mounting emotional turmoil. My feet were tucked up under me, and I had my head lying on the back of the couch, staring up at the white ceiling.

The silence was starting to annoy me. I didn't think I could take it anymore, so I looked up at Joel, who I caught staring at me.

"What?" I asked.

"Can we talk now?"

"You could have talked to me the whole time we were setting up," I said haughtily.

"Em. I know you're mad at me, but I need to explain some things."

"I am pissed, but I am also just embarrassed, disappointed, I don't know." Letting my guard down because I was tired, I told him how I truly felt.

"Well, I think what I have to say will make you and me both feel better." Joel scooted towards me on the couch and put his hand on my knee.

I stared at his muscular hand on my knee, and I felt a lightning bolt of chills run down my spine.

"K, spill Joel. Go on."

He took a breath and blew it out long and slowly. "Well, I was in my head all night. I am always around you. And I should have just ignored your brother and done what I wanted, but I couldn't, and now I need to explain."

"Yeah, you're not doing so well. Start over." I said, utterly confused.

He took another breath.

"Yeah." He huffed and then said, "I just don't know where to start. Let me think a moment."

"Okay?" I said. He sat there, still with his hand on my knee. The shivers were still running down my spine, but looking at him and then looking at his hand, I felt like he needed courage. A boost to help him get the words out.

I laid my right hand on top of the hand that grasped my knee, and I squeezed it. Joel looked down, and a smile graced his face. It made him look utterly remarkable.

He did another half-laugh and looked at me, “Emma, I really, really like you. I like you more than just as my best friend’s little sister. I have a huge crush on you.”

My heart skipped several beats.

“I was told by Everett the summer I visited before high school that I could never date you because it would be weird for him to have any of his friends date his little sister. He even told Lane, if you can believe that. He is super protective of you, and I think he also just didn’t want to lose any friends in case dating you never worked out. Anyway, I told him about how you asked me to the dance, and I said yes. He told me to watch it and not to try anything funny with you.” Joel half-laughed again, “The thing is, I have wanted to date you and I have been crushing on you since I met you that first time in your room. You were ten, and I was eleven. Back then, I was too shy, but now, I really don’t want to lose my friendship with your brother. He and I have become best friends since going to college together, and well, I guess I just made all of this too big of a deal tonight.”

We sat in another long, pregnant pause, and my mind went through every interaction Joel and I had ever had in our seven years of knowing one another.

“I was excited about tonight, just to be near you. But I did blow it. I’m sorry, Emma.”

“Thanks,” I said so quickly, I didn’t even know the words escaped my lips.

“So that is how I have been feeling.” Joel was nervous, but I had more questions.

“If you liked me all this time, what about dating Olivia last year and bringing her here last summer? And the first half this year? Or Sloan, when you were here the summer before eighth grade?”

“I mean, I liked them, yeah. I have had more girlfriends and hookups than that, I mean, I am in college. And I am not saying I am a man-whore. I am just. Damn, I think I am messing this up. Let me restart again. I have had other girls, and I’ve liked other girls, but I have not liked one nearly as much as I have ever liked you. Besides, I could ask you the same about Miles or James.”

“True. But you really like me?”

"Yes, Emma. I really, really like you. I wish I could be with you, but I really don't want to ruin my friendship with Ev. Or hell, any of the guys for that matter."

"I get that. But, well, I guess I should tell you that I like you too."

"I know. You haven't been the most subtle over the years. Which is probably why Everett said that to me."

"Oh. Whoops." Nervously laughing, I could feel my cheeks turn red like a tomato.

Joel reached up and grabbed my cheek, "Hey, don't be embarrassed."

I looked into his deep, dark green eyes, and my internal monologue told me, "fuck it."

I leapt from my spot on the couch and catapulted myself onto Joel's lap, and I smacked the biggest kiss on him. I expected him to pull away because I came at him like a bat out of hell, but he didn't. Instead, he wrapped his arms around me and deepened the kiss.

I felt every feeling and knew this moment was huge. I pulled away, "Joel, if I don't ever get to have you, then I will die very unsatisfied. We have one hour," I looked at the clock on the wall, "scratch that, we have maybe forty-five minutes tops for us to be together. And I want this. I want you. Even if it is the only time."

Joel's eyes went wide. "But, um, Emma, I think I am picking up a different meaning, and so maybe we should clarify what is going on and what you are thinking of."

"Damnit, Joel. I want you to have sex with me. If this is all I get from you in this life, I will take it. I'm saying I want you and you want me. But I don't want to get in the way of you and my brother, so if we have to do something in secret and keep it secret for the rest of our lives, I will. Thus, I want to get down and dirty with you, and then we can keep it a secret ... for the rest of our lives if that is what you wish."

"That is what I thought you were getting at. But Em, I don't want you to think this is all I want from you. I genuinely like you and have liked you for years. And well, I am not trying to get anything from you. I mean, I have a condom, but I mean, I have never—"

"Cool, we can do it. I think that is perfect. Don't you?" I felt relieved that he was a gentleman, but I wanted this. I had wanted this forever. I leaned down and kissed him lightly. I sensed he was nervous and unsure about this plan.

"Joel, I want to do this with you. I also want you to be in my life forever, even if that means we can't be together, and I only get to be around you because you are hanging around Everett, and our parents are summer friends. But I want, and I need this one moment. I need it for myself and for us. We should take this moment while we can and then hold on to it forever. Because it might be all we have."

"But what if I can't let you go after this? What if I want more?" He asked me.

I pushed some loose hair on his forehead back, because I knew what he meant. I smiled and kissed him again, not answering his question as we fell into our one moment of bliss.

3
joel

PRESENT DAY *(9 years after initial hookup)...*

I tapped out the last ever of my angry texts to my ex-step-sister, Marissa. She could go and get fucked for all I cared. I hoped she rotted in hell. After all the crap she and her dad put my mom and me through, my mom and I were finally done with this nightmare. A messed-up, horrible chapter was finally being closed. She was officially blocked, and I would have the lawyers send over a cease-and-desist and prepare the papers for a restraining order. After all Marissa did to my mom, me, Lola, and Everett, I vowed to take her down. Her latest claim was that our family owed her father and her money, and that they were co-owners of several businesses. Needless to say, she and her sleazy dad didn't have a leg to stand on. So I pretty much texted her to go to hell and then pressed the block button.

At least I could let that horrible part of my recent past go. It felt good not to deal with it.

When I was a senior in high school, my father died from a widow-maker heart attack. It upended my mom and my world. We were a close family. After that, my mother had to take the reins, leading all the business ventures, and I was next in line to inherit and take over. When I was a sophomore in college, my mom married Marissa's dad very quickly, and that was when things took a nosedive. I knew he was bad news, but Marissa was worse.

After Everett decided not to save Marissa and her father following my mother's divorce, Marissa thought I would be the one to save them. But little did she know, I hated her and him. They had tried every avenue to take my mother, my money, and my empire. But my mother had everything locked and ironclad. When she finally decided to divorce the loser, all his bad financial dealings came to light, and it wasn't looking pretty.

The thing that got me was that I never knew why my mom married him in the first place—and had stayed married to him for so long.

But now I was dealing with Marissa. She was relentless, telling me that she would expose my biggest secret if I didn't fund her lavish lifestyle. The thing was, what she thought was my biggest secret really wasn't. But I wouldn't let her know that. Otherwise, she would try to find something else to hold over my head.

I sat at my desk and turned to look out at the glowing New York City skyline. I really should have been home at my apartment, winding down for the night, but I had been staying later and later at work. I just couldn't bring myself to return to the place I had shared with the love of my life.

Lost in thought, I heard my phone ping. A text came through from Everett.

Everett: Hey, man! I'm in the city for the week. Meet me at Walla's now.

Me: Sorry, man. Can't.

Everett: Bullshit. Your mom told me you just sit in your office and mope. Meet me now. The driver is waiting.

Me: I just don't feel like being out. Sorry.

Everett: Come on, man. It's just me. It's been a minute since we hung out.

Me: I really don't want to. Maybe come to my place?

Everett: Too bad. Already here. See you in a few.

Fuck. I really didn't want to go out. Especially with Everett. Not because I was mad at him or anything, but because I couldn't bring myself to be around him, especially right now, as I was depressed and sad. But I got up, put on my game face, and headed to the car. Maybe seeing my best friend would be good for me. Anything to keep me from drowning in my own misery. Even though seeing him would bring up memories I didn't want to think of.

Twenty minutes later, seeing who was in that booth and heading to it, made me feel sick. Everett wasn't the only one I was meeting. Inside the booth were Lane, Piper, Lola, and finally Emma. I almost stopped, but kept walking and strode right up to the booth. Of course, the only spot left was right next to Emma.

"Finally. Where have you been hiding, bud?" Lane said.

"He has been the biggest sad panda. Or at least that is what his mom told me today." Everett said.

"Oh, I wonder why." Piper said with an air of knowing, "Why are you so sad, Joel?"

I stared at her, then at the rest of the group. Emma was looking down and fidgeting with a napkin, not meeting my eye. The sight of her ignoring me, ignoring me, instead of tempering my sadness, ignited a sharp flare of fury inside me. So I decided to play ball. After all, she was the reason I was this way.

"Great question, Piper. I was seeing someone, and then she decided to end things for no reason whatsoever. We had talks about everything. Hell, she had even moved a lot of her stuff into my place. But she backed out. And I have no idea why." I said angrily.

"Wait. You were seeing someone?" Everett said, shocked.

"Yes. But as I said, something happened, and she just ended things. And ya know what the shitty thing is, her stuff is still in boxes at my place. She won't come and get it. She won't even answer my calls or texts. Pretty sure she has blocked me, but I can't bear to just throw her crap out."

"What? Noooooooo." Lola said, disbelieving.

"Yes. It absolutely fucking sucks, guys." Addressing the group, including Emma.

"That does fucking suck. Sorry for your loss." Emma said, finally looking directly at me. Her green eyes showed no hint that she knew what I was talking about. Instead, they showed disinterest. So she wanted to play that game. Well, I could play chess, and I would checkmate her.

"Yeah. Well, hopefully one day my heart will heal, and I will find a new girl to bang and fall in love with. Right? Kind of like you are, Emma. Bouncing back so fast after every guy you've ever dated." She stilled. I knew I had hit the nail on the head.

"Are we missing something?" Piper asked as she looked between Emma and me.

"Nope. I think he is just jealous of how I bounce back so fast after breakups. Right, Joel?"

"Exactly," I said. Thankfully, the waiter showed up before I could say more of a retort.

"What will you be having, sir?"

"Macallan. Thanks." I said. I just needed a good scotch.

"Really going after it tonight, eh?" said Lane.

"Yup, you never know, I might see where the night takes me. Maybe it will take me into another pretty girl's arms." The drink was put in front of me, and I took a long swig. "So what has everyone else been up to?"

"Work." Said Everett and Lola simultaneously.

"Getting ready for the baby." Said Piper. She looked lovingly up at Lane, and you could just tell that they were soul-crushingly in love. I was happy for them. I looked at Emma and noticed she wasn't smiling. Good. Served her right.

"And you, Em?"

"Oh, ya know. Finally, getting my life together," she said.

"What do you mean by that?"

"Well, I am moving to Ireland at the end of this week, and so technically you are here for my going-away party."

This couldn't be happening. I knew Emma had been applying for jobs for fintechs, but I didn't think one would take her out of the US.

"Ireland? Wow. Did you get a new job?" I asked, followed by another swig of scotch.

"Yes. I will be the new Chief Technology Officer for a US-based fintech company, but they need someone to help lead their global tech team. So I will be stationed in Dublin."

"That's great, Em. When did you find out? I'm surprised I haven't heard anything from Ev." I said, trying to get more details, fearing that this was why she had left me.

"Shortly after the time of Piper and Lane's wedding. It took me a bit to accept, and then, I did. It's taken about six months to get my papers and everything set up. I have been working for them already for about three months, though. Learning as much as I can before I move."

"Well, congrats." Biting my tongue and trying not to sound hurt, I took another swig. "I am going to use the restroom." I stood up and walked to the back so I could collect myself.

I felt like punching the wall, but I got my hands wet at the sink and splashed water on my face. It all made sense now. The job—it was the fucking reason. The reason she left me. I had wanted to let everyone know that Emma and I had been hooking up and had been officially together for about a year. I was ready to take the step because I loved her. She even moved a majority of her stuff into my apartment. But then she just ended things without explanation, and I was left with nothing but her things.

I leaned up against the counter and took some breaths, trying to calm my racing mind and tone down my anger. How could she? Then the door opened, and in stepped Emma Manning herself.

"Hi. I thought-,"

"Emma, stop. Don't. You could have told me. We could have worked everything out. You didn't have to dump me for some job." I blew past her and went back to our friends. I couldn't speak to her, not while I was this pissed.

"So what did I miss?"

"Not much, I had the waiter bring you another scotch. Seems like you need it." Everett said.

"Thanks, man. I do. Work and the breakup have been awful."

Emma came back to the table, and I stood to let her back in. Her scent drifted to my nose. Vanilla, rose, and a hint of lemon. Her smell reminded me of home, elegance, and sunlight all in one. The smell brought back memories of us wrapped up in each other, the lingering smell after she showered, or me just kissing the top of her head in the morning after she brewed coffee. I didn't think I could do this. I couldn't sit next to her and pretend like nothing was happening between us.

Still standing, I turned and looked at my friends and Emma. "Uh, hey. Um ... I think I am going to go. I just, I just can't."

I turned and swiftly made it out of Walla's, then started walking down the street, calling my driver to come get me.

4
emma

LEAVING ABOUT thirty minutes after Joel, I walked into my apartment, shut the door, and fell against it, my body shaking with suppressed crying. Seeing Joel was rough, but having him find out part of the reason I was leaving, I could tell it undeniably crushed him. Sobbing uncontrollably, I wished I didn't have to do this, but I did because I was getting closer and closer to starting over and hopefully getting out from under the crushing weight of loving Joel Clarence.

I left my perch against the door and walked to my kitchen. I opened the fridge, took out the chilled bottle of wine, and started chugging it straight from the neck. I needed to numb myself because I felt like I had sold my soul for a job and gotten rid of my heart in the process. Stupidly, I thought of all the ways I should have and could have said no to this job. But I didn't, and now I was locked in. I didn't know how to get out of it, and I sure as hell wouldn't be asking Everett, my parents, or Joel for help even though Joel was probably the only one who could actually help me.

Did I need the job? No. Did I want this job and was so excited about it? Yes. It was my dream job. Was it all a black cloud now? Yes. I had royally fucked up. But I had to pick myself up by my bootstraps. I had a move to make this weekend, and I needed to start over.

But the thing nagging me was that I would still have the other reason I ended things with Joel hanging over me. I vowed to myself that I would find a way around that. Hopefully, by finding a new boyfriend or something, but I needed to make sure I moved on. Moving on was the only way I could heal.

I went into my room to start packing the rest of my belongings that needed to be shipped overseas or to my parents. Thankfully, I didn't have much since most of it was at Joel's.

Joel's.

I heaved out another long sob with just the thought of him and his apartment.

My phone pinged. I was startled because I wasn't expecting anyone to get hold of me.

Joel: You really didn't have enough faith in me that I would move mountains to be with you?

Joel: I would have gladly moved to Dublin, but you didn't even ask. You didn't even consult me on this decision.

Joel: After years of us hiding, I thought we were ready to be public. I was and still am ready to be with you. To do life with you. Why couldn't you just talk to me?

Me: Please stop. Don't make this harder than it already is for both of us.

Joel: Hard for both of us? It doesn't seem like it has been that hard for you. You ended it without even a discussion or an excuse. Tell me, did you just want to erase me and our past? Did the thought of actually going public scare you and make you realize you didn't want this? Just tell me. Please. I am going crazy not knowing why you left me.

Me: It's better for us. We were always a secret, and my life was changing. Yours wasn't. It's better to leave us in the past than move forward with a future.

Joel: No, it's not. That's bullshit.

Me: Please don't contact me anymore.

Me: Unless it is for an emergency with Everett, Lola, Piper, Lane, or my parents. Thanks.

Joel: Seriously, Emma?

I put my phone on silent and went back to packing my closet. I pulled down a photo box and opened the lid to take a look inside. And damn, this night couldn't get any worse. On top was a photo of Joel and me walking down the aisle at Piper's wedding. We looked so happy and good together. Little did both of us know that life-shattering things would be happening, and that it would tear us apart.

More wine down the hatch, I opened another box. It was full of little mementos that I had collected over the years. I pulled out a smooth rock, which was from the lake beach. I had picked it up after I had asked Joel to the dance and he had said yes. I sighed and put it back, pulling another memento out. It was a green four-leaf clover from a green boa I wore to that year's St. Patty's. It had fallen off and stuck to Joel's shirt. Later that night, he handed it to me and whispered delicately against my ear, "I am lucky you're mine."

Looking through the box, it was memento after memento, all tied to Joel. These boxes of memories would definitely be shipped to my parents. I couldn't destroy them, but I would not take them with me to my new life in Ireland.

I kept packing and drinking, packing and drinking until I could no longer feel my toes. I went to my bed, and I lay down. Remembering to do one thing that I probably shouldn't have done.

> Me: Please sand all my stufthings to my new add. You can call Ever to get it and send. I luy you.

Then I passed out.

A few days later, I landed in Dublin and was taken to the cottage by the sea I had bought. I had bought a 300-year-old thatched-roof cottage with a gorgeous view. Even though I was a chief technology officer and loved spending my time on a computer screen, I loved to unwind from the busy hustle of the tech world. The view was what sold me. Though the cottage was small, it was still bigger than my New York apartment, and the fun thing was that I had bought it all by myself with my hard-earned money and interest from my trust fund. My parents had no say and didn't help me. I had done it all myself.

When the driver pulled up, I saw what I had purchased, and I was in love. Just stepping out of the car, I knew I had done the right thing. For the first time in months, I felt an overwhelming sense of peace. This place was what I needed to heal. I needed this little cottage to mend my broken heart and soul.

The driver helped me deposit my suitcases inside. I had bought the place fully furnished. Seeing all that was there left me entranced. It was like I had walked into the coziest of places. There were wooden beams that helped support the rounded thatched roof. All of the furniture was stylish and made of wood. The other items and decor were full of old-grandma charm, making me feel like I'd stepped into my grandma's home in Pine Hills. I felt calm, soothed, and like this really was my home.

I walked out the back door to take a look at the sprawling sea, listening to the waves crash against the rocks below. It was peaceful.

Back inside, I looked into the makeshift garage. I had a Range Rover pre-purchased and delivered. I also had all of my pre-sent stuff put in the garage. Going out there, I had a hard time opening the garage door, but

I finally got it budged open. The garage was overflowing with my things, and the car barely fit underneath it all. But it was all there. Standing and staring at the overwhelming amount of boxes, I knew I needed to start getting things out of my car and into my house. I still had to go and get groceries and any other items I might need for my new home. I took a large box and hauled it from the garage to the main house. Setting it down, I realized that this was going to be a lot of work, and I wasn't as prepared as I thought.

5
emma

1 MONTH IN DUBLIN...

My job and new cottage kept me extremely, blessedly busy, and boy, was I grateful. Throwing myself into learning the new company I worked for, establishing myself as a strong female Chief Technology Officer, and trying to be social with my new coworkers was a thankful and welcome distraction from my feelings.

On top of that, my cottage kept me busy with unpacking, shopping for the cottage, and decorating. With my cottage being over 300 years old, there was a lot of work that needed to be done. A good chunk of the interior had been updated to be more modern, but there were some things I needed to do that the previous owner did not.

In the course of a month, I had gotten the electrical and some plumbing updated. I had the roof redone to still be "thatched". The goal was a roof that was fire-resistant, insulated, and yet still maintained that Irish Cottage charm. The "thatcher" who came to help me preserve the cottage's integrity was wonderful, and I ended up learning more about thatched roofs than I would have assumed many people did.

Even though I was eyes deep in spreadsheets, dust, and boxes, I was thrilled that my new home was allowing me this project and the opportunity to keep my mind squarely focused. The work at both work and home had me falling into bed at the end of the evening, and I would immediately fall asleep. It was a blissful, temporary numbness that made it so I didn't have to let my thoughts drift towards Joel, or my secret, or why I ended things.

More than anything, this month of distraction helped lessen the painfully throbbing heartbreak I had inflicted on Joel and myself. Now, it hurts, but it wasn't like a knife stabbing. It was more like breaking a bone, painful if we were looking at degrees of pain. More than anything, it was a pain that I was learning to cope with. And I had every faith that the pain would ease even more over time.

One of my new favorite things was going to see all the local shops in Dublin on Saturdays. This Saturday, I was buying stuff specifically for my guest room that I knew Joel would more than likely sleep in at some point. The thought of him here was a fragile, private hope I could never extinguish. The constant daydreams of him walking with me and picking out things didn't stop. Though it would be a long time before that happened, I knew that at some point, he would be at my cottage because of our group of friends and the fact that he had just always been a part of my life. I

I had been avoiding this particular room because I knew it would be perfect for him. It had an expansive, rich view of the sea and would be the perfect size for him to sleep and get some work done. It was cozy, masculine, and just had a spirit about it that it was for a male. But because of the pain, I had been putting it off and putting it off. Piper and Lane had a guest room, Everett and Lola's were almost done. Hell, even my office and the other guest rooms were completed. But this room was just hanging out until I could think of Joel and the past without sobbing.

The cutest antique shop, *Martin Fennelly Antiques,* was my go-to place this morning. They had furniture that I was dying to look at that I thought would really fit the feel and soul of what I was calling "Joel's

Room". Even though I should balk at calling it Joel's, I couldn't help myself.

Walking in, I was overwhelmed by the sense that pieces were calling out to me, begging me to take them home. I walked through and was immediately drawn to two inkwells. They were Edwardian, circa 1900. I immediately thought one would be perfect for Joel's desk and another for Lane and Piper's room, since Piper and Lane were both writers. I also came across a 19th-century Killarneyware Jewelry Casket that I could see Joel using to store his watch, wallet, and other items. He always dropped his stuff in a bowl at this apartment in New York. This could be a more historical and traditional place for him to discard his items.

I wandered through, roaming and picking out Killarney tables for the home and other needs. But it wasn't until I left that I had a sudden need to go into another hidden jewelry store that I would have missed if I hadn't had a powerfully nagging pull to look down a small alleyway. A sign hung above the only door in the alley walkway. *Clan Dagh Jewelry* was the name, and it was beckoning to me.

Directing myself down the alley and then going in through the door, I headed straight to the jewelry case by the register. In this case, there were hundreds of rings, necklaces, and earrings. Other jewelry was there, but only one piece spoke to me. Surrounded by other Claddagh rings that had emeralds, one stood out. It was like it was shouting from the rooftops, "Pick me! Pick me!"

This Claddagh ring was gold with a Ruby inside. The ruby just happened to be my birthstone. Seeing this ring, it felt like an undeniable fate. A voice cleared behind me, and I swung around quickly, startled out of my trance.

"Hello, lass. Would you like to try it on?"

"Oh- ah- yes," I said to the short-statured woman with grey hair. She pushed past me and went around to the other side. Before I even told her which one I wanted to look at, she pulled it out of the case and handed it to me.

It was like she was a mind reader and peered deep into my soul.

"Wow, um, thanks." I said, taking the ring from her, "I hope it fits."

"It will. They always fit." She smiled at me with a knowing smirk.

She continued, "This is a rare find." It dates from the early 19th century. Do you know much about the Claddagh ring? Or the history behind them?"

I hadn't put it on yet, but I looked up at her, "No, not really. I had a college roommate who had one. I know there is a way to wear it based on whether you're single or not."

"Aye. Yes. Well, I suggest you look it up. I think it will help you. But just know that the meaning is loyalty, friendship, and well ... love."

Staring at her, I finally looked back at the ring. It just seemed like this ring was meant for me. I slid it on my finger.

And by luck, magic, or true fate, the ring fit perfectly.

6
emma

THE 35TH DAY IN DUBLIN...

Dublin on a Sunday morning was something I had not expected to love as much as I did. There was a softness to it. A gentleness that New York never had. New York woke up swinging with horns and sirens and the relentless grind of eight million people all needing to be somewhere immediately. Dublin was more like Pine Hills. It woke slowly, as if it were stretching its arms, yawning, deciding to be beautiful at its own pace. I had walked every Sunday morning along the cliff edge to take in the fresh air and the salty, clean smell of the sea.

I told myself I walked because it cleared my head before a brand new week of work started. That was partially true.

The fuller truth was that walking was the only thing that made the weight in my chest feel even remotely manageable.

I pulled my coat tighter and looked at my new ring. It glinted in the morning sunlight while the sea was grey and restless this morning, the way it got when a change in weather was coming. The restlessness felt honest. It felt like the turbulent emotions I kept locked away.

I had been in Dublin for exactly thirty-one days.

I knew the exact number because I had been counting. Not in a hopeful way—not like counting down to something good. More like a person who had survived something and needed to keep track of how far they had gotten from it. Thirty-one days since I landed. Thirty-one days since I walked into my cottage and felt, for one pure and uncomplicated moment, like maybe I was going to be okay.

The grief came in waves, the way everyone always said it did, and I had always thought that was a cliché until I was living inside it. Some mornings, I woke up to almost quiet. A dull ache, manageable, something I could work around. And then other mornings I would stand in my kitchen waiting for the kettle to boil and something completely ordinary would happen. The light coming through the window at a certain angle, or a song drifting in from somewhere outside, or simply nothing at all—and it would hit me like a physical blow. It felt like a door swinging open into my very soul.

On those mornings, I did not get dressed. I just sat with it.

But on Sundays, I walked.

The lane curved, and I followed it, my boots quiet on the wet stone. A cat watched me from a windowsill with the supreme indifference that only cats and older adults could manage. I almost smiled.

Almost.

The thing about grief that nobody warned you about was the guilt that came wrapped inside it. I had expected sadness and braced for the loss. What I had not expected was the relentless, grinding guilt that had taken up residence somewhere between my ribs and refused to leave. I had not expected so much regret ...

There were things I could not stop turning over in my mind, no matter how many Saturday walks I took or how many hours I logged staring at the Irish Sea.

The first was the simplest and somehow the cruelest.

I hadn't known.

Fourteen weeks. I had been fourteen weeks along, and I hadn't known. I had missed two periods and chalked it up to stress. We had been so busy, Joel and I, so full of plans and the dizzying anticipation of finally going public. Plus, Piper and Lane had just married. I felt fine. I felt better than fine. It was like my life was finally clicking into place after years of waiting for it to. And all the while there had been a baby growing inside me I didn't know about, that I didn't protect, that I didn't take care of.

I stopped walking.

I pressed my hand flat against the stone wall of the lane and breathed.

It was something I had to be careful with. That particular spiral had a bottom I couldn't always find my way back up from. My therapist, the one I had started seeing via video call from Dublin, the one who did not know the whole story yet because I could not say it all out loud in one sitting, had told me that not knowing was not the same as not caring. That my body had not failed me. That these things happened and no amount of vigilance could have changed the outcome.

I heard her voice saying it clearly. I believed my therapist approximately sixty percent of the time.

The other forty percent of the time, I stood at stone walls in Dublin lanes, or leaned over on the cliffside by my house and tried to remember how to breathe.

I kept walking.

The second thing, the one that sat quieter but cut deeper, was the joy. That over-encompassing joy.

I was so happy when I found out. That was the part I could barely stand to revisit, because it felt like a cruelty now, like the universe had shown me something extraordinary and then snatched it back before I had even fully registered what I was holding. I remembered sitting on the edge of my bathtub in my New York apartment at six in the morning, staring at that test, and feeling something open up in my chest that I did not have a word for. Not just happiness. Something bigger and steadier than happiness. Something that felt permanent.

I had thought—and this was the part that made me feel the most foolish, the most naive —I had actually thought, in that moment, that it was all finally falling into place. Joel and I were going to go public. We were going to move in together. And now this. It felt like the universe confirming what I already knew, that we were right. That we had always been right.

Three weeks later, I was lying in a hospital bed, and I was no longer pregnant. Joel did not know any of it had ever happened.

I sometimes wondered if joy made grief worse. If letting myself feel that much happiness before I had any right to count on it was its own kind of recklessness. My therapist said that was not how it worked, that the joy was not the problem. That I was allowed to have felt it.

I was working on believing that, too. I needed to believe it.

The lane opened up, and I found myself at the small overlook where I had started coming on these walks. There was a stone railing above a short drop to the rocky shoreline, the sea spreading out wide and grey and enormous in front of me. I put my hands on the railing and looked out.

The third thing was Joel.

It was always Joel.

I had robbed him of a choice. That was the plainest way I could say it to myself, even though it made me feel sick. He deserved to know. He deserved to grieve with me, or to try to help, or to be angry, or to feel whatever he would have felt. But I had taken it all from him without asking. I decided for him he was better off not knowing, and I had dressed it up in my head as protection, as love, as sparing him. But underneath all of that, the truth was simpler and uglier than I wanted to admit.

I was terrified. Not of Joel's reaction. Joel would have come. Joel would have dropped everything, driven through the night, held my hand through every terrible appointment, and never made me feel like a burden for a single second of it. I knew that. I had always known that.

What I was terrified of was what came after.

If he had been there and if he had sat beside me in that doctor's room and held that photo of the embryo and heard the words holoprosencephaly spoken aloud by a doctor who was very kind and very sorry, I think it would have become real in a way I was not sure I could survive. Not the loss itself. I had already lived through that. But the look on his face. The grief in his eyes. The way he would have looked at me afterwards, with all of that love and all of that sorrow, and I would have known that I had done this to him. Given him something and taken it away in the same breath. That it had been mine to carry, and somehow I had pulled him into it.

I thought I was protecting him.

I thought I was protecting myself.

Looking out at the grey Irish Sea on my thirty-first morning in Dublin, I was starting to understand that I had mostly just been protecting the version of our story I could not bear to lose. The version where we were happy and ready and everything was clicking into place. The version where I had not spent fourteen weeks not knowing. The version where my body had not done what it did.

I was protecting the story. And in doing so, I had left him alone in his own version of the story.

A gull cried somewhere overhead, and I watched it arc across the sky and disappear. The sea moved the way it always did — indifferent and enormous and completely unbothered by any of this.

I pushed off from the railing and turned back toward the lane.

Thirty-one days.

I did not know how many more it would take. But I kept walking, one Sunday at a time, with the weight of all three things sitting in my chest, and the slow, stubborn hope that one day the weight would be something I could carry without stopping to press my hand against a wall and remember how to breathe.

I was not there yet.

But Dublin was patient with me. And the sea was always there when I needed something bigger than myself to look at.

And thirty-one days was farther than thirty.

That would have to be enough for now.

Weeks Later...

What I had not expected was the regret in leaving Joel. That came strongly during my second month in Dublin. It was a constant, sharp undertow, pulling me back to the moment I broke us. It wasn't the Dublin job, though that was the excuse I'd given. The job was the key to this new life, my shield against the old one, but it was just a symptom of the real problem, the secret I couldn't breathe a word of. I had left him to protect him from a truth I feared would destroy his carefully built world, but in doing so, I'd destroyed mine.

This secret wasn't a choice; it was a consequence. It was a fragile, terrifying reality that had formed in the silence of our hidden moments, a life-altering force I hadn't dared to share. Had Joel known, his life would have been violently upended. And I wouldn't do that to him. Not even for my own happiness. It was the ultimate act of loyalty, twisted into the cruelest betrayal.

I knew I had to move forward. My only refuge was the cottage. I finally stood in the guest room, the one with the expansive view of the wild, churning sea. The one I stubbornly called "Joel's Room." It was a quiet rebellion, this space I was dedicating to him, a place he didn't know existed. And here it was, full of boxes from my house and my parent's house. I had to face the boxes.

My heart felt like a dull, heavy stone as I knelt and opened a long, flat box I hadn't touched since the shipper dropped it. Inside, nestled in tissue paper, was the white rose boutonniere from the dance, dried and brittle, and next to it, the ridiculous, floppy green boa from the St. Patty's bar crawl. The boa's four-leaf clover was pinned to the tissue beneath it. "I am lucky you're mine," his voice echoed in my memory, as clear as the sea-spray hitting the windows.

The grief was a wave, and this time, it nearly capsized me. I slammed the box lid shut. *Stop it, Emma. You have a room to decorate.*

I forced myself to my feet, my new Claddagh ring catching the dim Irish light. Heart facing in—taken, but to whom? I was tied to a ghost, a memory, a man I'd pushed away with the love of a lifetime. I inhaled deeply and turned the ring outwards. Because even though my heart would always be Joel's, I wasn't taken.

The next box was full of tools and personal effects. A small, heavy, metal desk organizer. I picked it up. A flash of memory: Joel, in his New York office, dropping his father's old watch into it after a long day. It was a small, intimate detail of a life I was no longer a part of, and the pang of loss was so fierce it buckled my knees. He used this when visiting my house.

A text pinged, breaking the silence. It wasn't Joel, but Everett.

Everett: Heard from Mom. She's worried about your cottage roof. Everything okay? We should all plan a trip soon. Dublin needs a Pine Hills takeover. Lola is dying to see you.

A small, genuine smile finally touched my lips. The Pine Hills family circle was still intact, even with my absence.

Me: Roof's fixed. Thatchers were amazing. Dublin is lovely. Tell Lola I said hi. And yes, a takeover sounds amazing. Just... not yet. I am not ready for everyone. Maybe you and Lola can just come for a weekend?

I put the phone down. The "not yet" was a promise I was making to myself. Not yet until the bone was fully set. Not yet until I had a plan for the impossible secret. I looked around the empty room, then at the boxes of my things. This room, this whole cottage, was the quiet war I was fighting. A war to build a future I could live in, even if it was one where I was perpetually alone and only warring with myself.

7
joel

THREE MONTHS.

Three months had passed, each day a razor-wire slice of hell.

Three frustrating, depressing, horrible months had gone by. I was severely depressed, angry, vengeful, heartbroken, and sad. The list went on, each word described a wound I had in me. My soundtrack consisted of sad songs, with "my tears ricochet" by Taylor Swift on repeat. I had succumbed to being a Swiftie because her songs spoke to me and perfectly scored this fiery hell I was in. The despair I felt was unlike anything else. It was as if Emma had shredded my heart like pulled pork. Half of my body was missing. My soul had been sheared from my body, leaving me a vacant, walking zombie. If this was what losing Emma was like when we weren't even official, I couldn't imagine losing her with everyone knowing. This breakup was fucking awful.

And the worst part was that the only person I wanted to talk about this with and lean on was her. Not her brother, not Lane—her.

I played All I Want by Kodaline on repeat as well. The line, "*If you loved me, why'd you leave me?*" played in my mind over and over like a broken record, the needle skipping on the best part of the song.

I told my mother I would be taking some time off and that I wanted to travel. I asked Everett for Emma's address so I could send her flowers and a care package. Or at least that is what I told him. Instead, I sent over everything that was Emma's. I wanted nothing in my apartment reminding me of her. The ghost of her vanilla, rose, and lemon scent haunted every room. Hell, I was about to put my entire apartment up for sale just to erase even the memory of her in here.

I had one box left to send, and it was sitting on my kitchen counter, staring at me. Its cardboard edges looked like accusing fingers. I needed to send it off before I left for a long vacation in the south of France. But the damn thing had me in a crosshair. It was beckoning me to open it. Taunting me that if I looked inside, all my worries would dissipate. Not being the bigger person over a fucking box, I grabbed a kitchen knife and sliced the tape open.

The lids popped open. I hesitated to look in and immediately thought about re-taping it. But curiosity got the best of me, and I had already come so far. I peeked over the cardboard flaps and saw a wooden box atop several sweaters. It was small, dark, and ancient-looking. I knew I shouldn't, but the second box needed to be opened too.

Lifting it out of the cardboard box, I held the ornate wooden box in my hands. Looking at it more closely, it seemed to be an Irish memory box. The pyrographed triskeles were intricate. I knew from memory that this box had been passed down to Emma from her mother's Irish mother.

Moving the latch to the side and flipping the cedar box open, I saw the contents. My hand flew to my mouth, and tears immediately filled my eyes. As a man, I don't think I have ever been so overcome with emotion. This shock was a physical blow, knocking the breath from my lungs.

Inside was nothing I ever expected to see. The wooden keepsake held something I should have known about. That Emma should have told me about. But I was finding out because I snooped into the last box remaining at my apartment.

Was it fate that I found this?

Was it divine intervention? A sick joke?

Inside was a positive pregnancy test and a photo of an embryo. I lifted both to inspect the items in more detail. The photo was time-stamped for a month after Lane and Piper's wedding. It was labeled with the embryo's age: 14 weeks.

Emma had been or was pregnant with our baby. And she didn't say a damn fucking word.

Why?

My mind went to a million different memories, thinking of why she didn't tell me. And it struck me that we had been so happy, then she had gotten really sick in October. I told her I would meet her at the hospital, but by the time I got there, she was being released and said it was just a bad stomach bug. They gave her an IV and sent her on her way.

But could it have been something else? Morning sickness?

My mind then went to a dark place that said maybe this baby wasn't mine, and that was why she didn't tell me. But I had been hooking up with Emma since I was twenty. And we had been exclusive for the last two years. There was no way it could be anyone else's.

Emma was my person, and I was hers. She was my soul, my heart. And I knew deep down that I was hers. The answer was staring at me from the tiny photo. A baby was what had to do with why she left me and moved across the fucking Atlantic.

I couldn't stand it, so I called her.

*Ring ... ringing...ring...*voicemail.

I dialed again.

*Ring ... ringing...ring...*voicemail.

I dialed again.

I dialed ten more times before finally leaving a voicemail. My hands were shaking with a mix of fury and desperate hope.

After I heard her message, I said, with unshed tears, "Em. I know. I know. Why couldn't you have told me? Why did you hide it? Just tell me. Please." I ended the message sobbing like I was a five-year-old boy once again who had thrown a baseball through the window, which had actually happened.

I stood there, staring at the box, the test, and the photo. I didn't know what to do but cry, and I had no one to turn to. This was so fucked.

Hours or what seemed like hours later, I made my decision. I would still go to France. I would get some distance from all of this, try to heal, and give her the space to do the same. But first, I would write a note and send this particular box overnight to Emma. She needed to see what I had found; I needed to speak my piece. I needed to get out my thoughts and feelings without being diminished, interrupted, or lied to. So I went to my office, pulled out the stationery my mother had gifted me years ago, a heavy cream card stock with my initials embossed on the top, and wrote the longest love letter of my life. It would be my last plea.

8
emma

6 MONTHS *in Dublin and 7 Months A.B. (After Breakup)...*

Kicking ass and taking names was the game I was playing. At work I was crushing it. Being a CTO was not something I ever dreamed about, but it was what I became and I was damn good at it. I was a big thinker and this job really fit my skills and wheelhouse.

Speaking of houses, my house was almost perfect. I was still looking for the perfect pieces for "Joel's Room." But every time I went in there, I couldn't finish it. I'd bought a few items and put them in there, but nothing was in order. Not only that, but I had received the boxes from Joel. Almost four months after I moved to Dublin, the last boxes arrived that had been hanging out at his apartment in NYC arrived. I didn't have the heart or energy to go through the boxes, so I just piled them into the room I knew he would one day sleep in.

Today, though, I swore I would at least get the bed made up and the nightstands in place, just in case I had a lot of visitors come calling. More than anything, I just needed to work on it. So I went in. But before I could get even remotely started, I was literally saved by the bell. My doorbell.

Hurrying down my downstairs hallway and heading to my front door, I was thinking it was just a delivery driver delivering something I forgot I bought. I opened my heavy wooden door, and lo-and-behold, there was Piper.

"OH, MY GOD! PIPER?" I screamed.

"BESTIE!" Hugging me tightly, Piper pushed us into my house.

"What are you doing here?" I asked, still reeling in shock.

"I am here for a mini vacay away from Lane. I also have a few book signings here in Ireland. But really, I am just vacationing and thought I'd see you."

"Oh my gosh! This is amazing!" Hugging her again tightly. I don't think I realized how much I needed her — or really anyone from home. Hugging her brought me a sense of peace I hadn't felt since I first looked at the sea when I got to my cottage in Dublin.

Tears came out like the river scene in The Lord of the Rings. A gushing wall of water ran down my cheeks.

"Hey, hey. What is going on?" Piper asked, pulling away and smoothing my hair. She grabbed my face in her hands and pointed my head to look at her. "Emma. What's up?"

"I think I really fucked up."

"About moving here?"

No ... with Joel."

"Ah," It was all she said. It let me know she knew about us. "Let me get settled. Maybe you can open a bottle of wine, and we will kick off this vacation with you telling me everything."

"Thanks, Pipes. Sorry. You just go here. But I think I needed this, and I didn't realize it until you were at my door."

"Let's call it luck and fate. I was meant to be here. Now let me pee and throw my bags in the guest room."

Sitting on the couch in my sunroom, I looked out the expansive windows to the churning sea and the rolling waves beyond. For the first time in months, I felt a sense of calm wash over me as I decided to tell Piper everything.

"I am going to ask that you just sit there and listen. And also, please keep the wine flowing. It will help me get through everything." I paused and then continued, "So Joel and I started hooking up when I was nineteen..."

After recounting the early years of Joel's and my relationship. Piper asked for a break to get another bottle. Detailing the years and how we had only been officially exclusive for a few of the last years, I was gearing up for the big ending.

Piper came back with a new bottle of Cabernet, opened it, and topped my glass off.

"Emma, I wish you had felt like you both could have told us. I'm so sorry you guys had to keep it a secret for so long. No wonder you both are so unhappy right now."

"It wasn't you. Everett had threatened Joel way back in the day, and I think we both just got comfortable with us two being the only ones knowing."

"Everett can fuck off. He is one to talk, dating Lola in private for so long. And she is one of your best friends."

"True. But besides all that, this is the real reason Joel and I ended things. I actually ended things. And I think I shouldn't have. But I just couldn't look at him without feeling ... without feeling shame ..." I sobbed again.

"Aww, hun, what happened? Did Joel do something?"

I choked out, "No. I did. Or, well, my body did. Joel and I were going to announce, right after your wedding, that we were together. I was so happy.

On top of that, I had found out I was pregnant with Joel's baby. And I was over the moon. It felt like all the chips were falling where they were supposed to. And then, a week before Joel and I were going to ask you all over so we could share the news, I went to the doctor. I thought I was only maybe five or six weeks along, but I was actually fourteen weeks. Fourteen weeks and I had no idea. No symptoms besides missing my period for only two months. But when I went to the doctor, they rushed me through all these tests. Abnormalities had shown up on the ultrasound. I thought about calling Joel, but I was so stunned just to be that far along. We went through every test imaginable, and I could tell the doctors were concerned.

"The rest is a blur, but I had scheduled a D&E with the doctor as it was confirmed by the doctor that the baby had holoprosencephaly, or in layman's terms, "the brain failed to divide." I was scheduled to have a D&E, and then the next thing I knew, I was miscarrying. I had miscarried our child. And I broke.

"I didn't know what to do, so I told Joel and everyone that I was at a job interview, but really I was at my house in Pine Hills and grieving. When I finally resurfaced, I broke up with Joel, who, by the way, had most of my things because we were also planning to move in together in New York, and well, I just left. Thankfully, I had gotten a job here and left. But all the hurt from the loss of the baby, and then adding more on because of dumping Joel, well, it has been eating at me. Slowly. And I haven't told a soul. Instead, I have numbed myself with work, whiskey, and random pub men. There is just an ache in me that won't go away. And I think the only way I can heal is telling Joel. But I just can't. I can't crush him even more."

"Oh Em. I am so sorry." Hugging me tightly, Piper just let me cry on her shoulder, while I let the last seven months of hurt and grief flow out of me.

After crying for about five minutes, I pulled away from Piper, and I looked back out the window. Through puffy eyes, something glinted by the frame of the window. Popping up off the couch, curiosity got the best of me, and I wandered over to see what it was. Between the window sill and the window frame, a gold piece of metal was sticking out. I pulled it lightly but couldn't get a grip. I went over to a tiny desk with some sewing tweezers, and grabbed them to help me pull out whatever it was.

"What are you doing, Emma?"

"There is something here." I pulled again, and a tiny gold metal pendant was unearthed.

It was a triskele. There were several meanings for the triskele, but after all that I had shared with Piper, it was cosmic or divine that this was presented to me in my home. It was like the cottage had a ghost or something, leaving me little notes—moving me forward on my journey. This triskele, I knew, meant life, death, and rebirth.

"What is it Em? You look like you've seen a ghost."

"I think I have one or a spirit that is watching out for me. It left me a triskele. And I think it is telling me that it is time for rebirth. Time for me to restart."

9
everett

8 OR SO MONTHS AFTER *Joel and Emma were dumb and broke up, or whatever ...*

I was in Munich trying to get Joel off his moping ass to go fight for my sister. We all had kind of pieced together that they were fucking around. And I was here to mend everything, because without them together, it was putting a damper on the rest of us.

So I pretended I had work and headed across the Atlantic to Germany to help him get his head and heart back in the game. I figured he just needed to get it all off his chest. So I came to Munich so he could finally move on, get over himself, and get back with Emma. Plus, Lola and Piper told me to.

Though honestly, I thought that maybe, just maybe, I was the reason they were no longer together or doing whatever it was they were doing. A long, long time ago, way back when we were kids, I told Joel to never date my sister, or I would kick his ass. But we were just kids.

And I was one to talk. I had secretly dated Lola, and now I was in love and going to spend the rest of my life with Lola. Lola was one of

Emma's best friends. So I couldn't judge. I wouldn't judge. If this was why they broke up, I needed Joel to know that he and Emma dating was fine, and that I had no room to talk.

Seeing Joel and Emma together made me happy because they were happy. I had seen it over the years—the little moments when their worlds collided. Once when they were dancing at my parents' anniversary party, I swear they were looking at each other like they were the only ones in the room and the only ones the music played for.

Another time, at St. Patrick's, it seemed like they had secretly agreed and were going to announce that they were together, but they didn't. We could all see how much they enjoyed each other's company.

Then at Piper and Lane's wedding, I thought they would finally let us all in on their big secret, but they didn't. Even though you could swear they were going to announce they had secretly been married for years. But they just tiptoed around each other and snuck away at the same time when they didn't think any of us would pick up on the fact that they both had left at the same time, multiple times, not thinking any of us would pick up on it.

But then, Emma became sad, and I thought maybe Joel had dumped her. I was furious and wanted to confront him, but he was so distraught that I didn't. Lane and I kept extra tabs on him, while the girls kept tabs on Emma. I swore that whatever happened between them, it couldn't have been that bad. But the final time I saw them together at Walla's, well, it just seemed like they both were miserable in hell.

Then they both flitted off to different countries, leaving the rest of us to dance around their secret relationship. But, we were done tiptoeing and dancing around it. I was going to make them bring it all out wide into the open.

Joel and Emma were perfect for each other and needed each other. They were the perfect puzzle pieces that fit, or whatever the hell authors say in romance books nowadays. As Emma's big brother and Joel's best friend, I knew I needed to be the one to bring them together. The easiest way to do that was by talking to Joel over a good meal and a lot of scotch.

Essentially, I was going to kick Joel's ass with words, then pump him up to get his head and heart back in the game and fight for my sister. It was the least I could do. Also, Lola would kill me if I didn't try. And I wasn't about to face an angry Lola.

10
joel

8 MONTHS *of being miserable or as I called it, 8 months A.B. ...*

Germany was slowly growing on me. It was a far cry from Thailand, but I vowed to learn, help, and continue to grow. I was learning who I was as a man, and honestly, I think I needed it.

I grew up in luxury and never wanted for anything, but over the last few months I saw and experienced things that changed my worldview. It changed me at a soul level. I was helping set up our Germany office before I went to volunteer with some youth when my phone started ringing.

It was Everett.

We hadn't spoken much since I left. Even though he didn't know what happened between Emma and me, and it wasn't his fault we broke up, I had distanced myself. Seeing him or talking to him would bring up feelings that I didn't want him to question.

"Hey, Ev. What's up?" I answered.

"Hey, man. I'm in Germany, and I wanted to see what you're up to. Lane said you were here in Munich. You free tonight?"

"Tonight? You're here in Munich?"

"Yeah, you know how it is. Work."

"Uh, yeah, I get that. Um, is Lola with you?" I asked nervously. There was no way I could see both of them and not show how much I was hurting.

"Nope. Just me. So dinner?"

"Ya know, tonight is really-"

"Joel, you've been avoiding me—all of us. You're coming to dinner. I'll text your assistant to let you know where to go. See you later." He hung up on me. *Click.*

A few hours later, I was seated at Tantris, waiting for Everett to grace me with his appearance. The nerves I had made me arrive here a few minutes early. I was sweating bullets because I truly didn't know if I could bullshit with my best friend anymore.

A hand grasped my shoulder, and I looked up at Everett. He smiled, but his eyes looked a bit sad.

"Hey, man," I said.

"Hey. Get ready, I'm not pulling any punches."

Everett sat with his masculine billionaire air. What most people didn't realize was that even though we were both outrageously wealthy, we were also really normal. If you didn't know us, you really wouldn't know that we were part of the one percent. This was largely due to our parents and Pine Hills. Even though I was raised more in NYC, Pine Hills taught me to be humble and appreciative—Everett, more so, since he went to school and lived in Pine Hills pretty much full-time.

Thinking about it, my time in Thailand and Australia, and now helping kids here in Germany, have made me even more human.

"So I'm not going to dick around. You've been an ass for ignoring me and distancing yourself. So why?"

"Wow, you're not even going to get me drunk first? Talk about not beating around the bush."

"Sounds like you were in the Bush and Thailand, and now you're in a big city. So now that I can actually get a hold of you, you need to talk. What's goin' on?" He was hurt. And it made me feel worse.

"First off, I was in the Outback. The Bush is Australia's rural countryside. Get it right, dude. I'm not sure you'll find this helpful. But it doesn't have to do with you—well, it has to do a little bit with you. But I don't want to talk about it. I just need time. I'll be back to my normal self soon."

"That's bullshit, man. You've been sulking for months. We're best friends. Spill. I'm not letting you off the hook."

Everett glared at me like he was about to beat me to a pulp if I didn't start talking. I had no doubt he would beat me in the middle of this two-star Michelin restaurant. Then he would pay for all the damages or buy it outright. Maybe he already owned it, and that was why he brought me here — to pulverize me.

"I don't know if I can." Staring back at him.

"Do it. Try me."

I took a breath, and downed the scotch I had been nursing. Signaling for another one to the waiter who had been eyeing us the whole time, I wouldn't talk until I had another full drink. Waiting, Everett stared me down. Like he would wait patiently until I spoke. Like he had all fucking night. I wasn't getting out of this conversation. But maybe it was time to just get it over with.

My drink was deposited in front of me by the server. Taking a swig and letting out a long sigh, I started, "Well, you're sister, and I have been dating officially and exclusively for a few years, and fucking for over nine."

Everett didn't blink.

"And we didn't come forward because we didn't want the friendship between you and me to be ruined. But when I asked Emma to go public and say fuck it, she dumped me. Then she went to Ireland. So there it is. I am a fucking goddamn mess, and fucking ripped apart. That's why I left and have been soul-searching. Doing a walkabout or whatever. I'm trying to get my shit together and also try to figure out if I can ever get over your little sister. Fuck." I slammed my fist and leaned back in my chair.

"I figured that was it. But I didn't want to pry. Figured you or Em would say something sooner or later." He said, leaning back in his chair and taking a drink.

"You knew?"

"We all guessed something was going on. I'll admit, I didn't think it was going on for that long. I only kind of guessed when I had been secretly dating Lola. We thought it started then. And really, man, I didn't think much of it. I was dating Lola in secret. How could I be upset with you for doing the same?"

I huffed. That was for damn sure. Everett kept his relationship secret. So it really wasn't fair of him to expect the same of Emma and me. I had said as much to her about a week before she dumped me. She seemed to be on the same page, but then she broke up with me. And after viewing the insides of the box, I was almost a hundred percent sure I knew why.

"Has Emma said anything... to anyone?"

"I know Piper saw her, and I think she might have said something to Piper. But I can't be certain."

I hummed an agreement.

"I wish I hadn't told you to stay away from her when we were young. It was stupid, but we were kids. If anything, I should have said something when I suspected you two were hooking up. I should have let you know it was okay. I'm sorry, Joel."

He looked so sincere. And it helped me feel a bit better. Nothing could heal my heart after Emma shattered it, but maybe hearing an apology from my best friend was one step in the right direction.

"Thanks, man. I think I needed to hear that." I said.

"Now, I am going to say something you probably don't want to hear."

Shit. He was probably going to tell me Emma had moved on to some Irish guy. I didn't think I was ready to hear it. But he was going to tell me anyway. My stomach dropped, and it felt like I was about to be kicked in the balls.

"You need to go and fight for her. She isn't happy either. You belong together, and you both need to pull your heads out of your asses and figure it the fuck out."

Not what I was expecting, but I would take it.

"She broke up with me."

"Yeah, and it was fucked up. Emma is depressed. And if I know my sister, she is regretting it. So instead of both of you being miserable maybe you should talk and reconnect. Get over yourselves. And, I can't believe I'm going to say this because Emma is my sister, but maybe you two just need to get laid ... with each other." Everett let out a dry heaving sound after he said the words.

"You're saying to get over her, I need to get under her?" I said with a laugh.

"Unfortunately. But come on, you two are perfect for each other. Stop denying the invisible string that binds you two together. And if anyone knows about love and meant to be and all that shit, it's me. So take my advice, get your shit together, go after her, and be together."

"Sounds so easy."

"It is. You just gotta get your head out of your ass." He said.

I thought I had, but he was right. I needed to stop fighting our connection and fight for her—to be with her. I just need a solid plan.

11
joel

1 YEAR ***and 1 month A.B. ...***

My office was quiet here in Munich. The only sound was the faint hum of the flor*Ring, ring... ring, ring... ring, ring... Hello, this is Everett Manning. Please leave a message after the beep.*

"Hey, man. I have a plan, and I need you to call me back ASAP. Thanks." I said.

Five minutes later ... I was on the line with Everett, "Hey, Ev. Thanks for calling back so fast."

"No problem. What's up, man?"

My heart hammered in my chest with the thought of what I was going to ask Everett. "I need help getting Emma back. I was thinking about going to her for St. Patty's, and I was wondering if you and Lola might be able to join, kind of make it seem like we were going for a friend's St. Patty's getaway."

"Sure can do. I'll run the logistics passed Lols and see what she says. But I am sure she will be down."

"You don't have any other questions? You're just on board."

"Nope. I am here to help and make sure you and my sister stop being sourpusses. I'm tired of you both moping. So whatever I gotta do, I'll fucking do."

"Thanks, man. I'll send more details. But can you just get Lola on board? I am going to do whatever it takes to get her back. And if I can get her back over St. Patrick's, then hopefully being in Ireland will give me some luck as I spend however long trying to win her back."

"I have faith that the luck of the Irish will be on your side. It's about time you get her back Joel."

And he was right. I hoped that luck would be on my side as I plotted my invasion into Dublin to win back the love of my life. I would do any fucking thing to have her be mine. I had been doing a lot of reading about Ireland and luck. St. Patrick's Day was not just a celebration; it was a potent symbol of new beginnings. For luck, I crossed my fingers, wishing for a new beginning with Emma.beginning.

12
emma

1 YEAR *and 2 months later, A.B. ...*

Dublin pubs were truly one-of-a-kind, and I had found that I loved them more than anything. They were the place I had made friends outside of my work, let loose, and even found a few Irish men to bed me —or at least try to bed me. But deep down, it all meant nothing. I was filling the gaping ravine that had split my heart into two. I was numb, working my dream job but hating it, and living in the most beautiful home and place and not enjoying it. Moving to Ireland and starting my new job as CTO of a fast-growing tech company was supposed to get me out of this funk and depression. It was supposed to heal me. Healing wasn't happening. Instead, I was masking my pain with casual flings, Guinness, and when those two things didn't work, I threw myself into work and only work. Work was the only thing that truly kept my mind off the past. It threw me into what the future could be like and into solving day-to-day problems and finding solutions. But here I was, at another Irish pub with my new friends, and eyeing the tall, tattooed Irish man ordering a beer at the bar. I sauntered over to him after a long swig of my beer, mustering the courage to approach this hunk of meat, when my phone vibrated in my back pocket. I reached back and looked at the screen to see my brother's name and face grace it. Groaning, I knew I had to take it, so I answered and headed out the front door to stand on the sidewalk.

"Hello, dear brother."

"Hey sis. How is Dublin?"

"Great! When are you and Lola coming to visit? Your room is waiting for you. I know it's only been a few months since your last visit here, but it would be nice to see you both."

"Soon. How does in three weeks sound?" Everett said, sounding extremely needy and pleading.

"Um, yeah! That would be great!"

"Sweet! I will tell Lola. We thought we would celebrate St. Patty's in Dublin because that would be the ultimate way to celebrate."

"Oh my gosh, I forgot it was coming up. Yeah! That will be super fun. I can't wait to see you two."

"By the way, we asked Lane and Pipes, but with them due soon, she can't travel. So it will just be Joel and us." My stomach dropped. Lola, Everett, and Joel? Emma stilled and tried to counteract her silence.

"Yuh-Yeah! That is great. Piper told me she was about to pop. I plan to head back to work from Pine Hills for a month or so after she gives birth. But it will be fun to see you, Lola, and Joel. How is he? Joel, I mean." She hadn't heard from him. It had been over a year since Joel had sent over all of the boxes, she assumed, from his apartment, but after the day he called her multiple times in a row, she hadn't heard from him. She should have answered the calls, but she was locked in a board meeting all day and couldn't. After that, she texted him to say she was sorry and that she would call him that weekend, but her text never went through. She assumed he had officially blocked her, and that had stung. She remembered going to the pub later that night and hooking up with her first random Irishman, which did nothing to heal her heart.

"Joel is good. He was in France, and now I think he is in Germany or Amsterdam? Something like that. But he said he would fly at the same time we would on Monday next week. I told him you had a room for him, and he said he would get a place, but I told him you would be pissed if he got a different place. So make sure your other room is ready for him. Anyways, do we need to bring anything from our parentals house?"

It was a lot to take in.

"Nope. Um, if I think of anything, I will let you and Lola know."

"Cool. Alright, baby sis. See you Monday. Be ready!"

"Oh, I will. Just remember, I am still working on Monday."

"Can you take off Tuesday since that is St. Patty's?"

"Yes. Everyone will be off that day. Our company is treating it like a national holiday. The beauty of working in tech is that I also have Wednesday off too. I will have to work Thursday and Friday, but how long are you staying?"

"Well, we were thinking of a few weeks? Lola's brother might join at some point, but we were thinking about looking at real estate for you to purchase. Lola has always dreamed of having an international cozy place. Or so she said. So I figured, why not Ireland?"

"Sure, why not. Um, well, make sure you guys bring some fancy stuff. If not, we can always go shopping. I do have some galas to attend over the next few weeks, and it would be nice if you could come with me. It would help put me on the map in Ireland."

"Can do, sis. Alright, I gotta go. See you in a few days. Love you."

"Bye. Love you too."

My mind whirled. Not only did I need to get ready to have Lola and Everett here for a few weeks, but my ex, Joel, would be staying at my place. Who knew how long he would be there, but he was still coming. Maybe the time apart since I broke up with him had healed him enough to be around me again. Did I think we could become friends again? No. Did I think this would be easy? No. But I had to play it cool and get ready for what I was sure would be the ultimate train wreck waiting to happen.

Heading back into the pub, I went up to the bar and strode up to plant myself next to the tattooed Irishman I had been eyeing earlier. My heart was racing, and my head was telling me I needed to find release and find someone to help ignore the fact that Joel would be coming to Dublin.

"Hi there," I said with bold confidence.

"Howya." He said.

"I saw you eyeing me earlier. Want to get out of here?" I didn't want any more small talk.

"You're not going to sweet-talk me first?"

"Nope," I said.

"How do you know I don't have a lass at home?"

"Because you have been eye fucking me all evening."

"So it's that easy with you?" He said.

"Not usually, but tonight I am granting you an exception."

"Well. I guess I'd better take you up on your offer."

"Good." I grabbed his hand and led him out of the bar. When we got outside the pub, I was tugged back by Mr. Tattooed Irishman.

"Can I get your name?"

Finally, taking a breath actually to have a conversation with this stranger, I looked up at him. He had dark eyes and long, wavy hair. He was good-looking in a long-haired Jamie Dornan kind of way. But he wore these square, dark-rimmed glasses that made him seem a bit more nerdy.

"I wasn't planning on giving it to you. But it is Emma. What's yours?"

"Emma. It suits you. Hi, Emma, I'm Grady."

"Grady...that suits you." I gave him a half-smile after using the same words he used on me.

We waited in silence for the taxi I had booked on FreeNow to arrive. It was comfortable, but it also made me realize I missed my comfortable silences with Joel.

And it made me realize that I probably shouldn't be taking Grady to my place.

As the taxi pulls up, I have a mental tug of war with my brain, should I–shouldn't I. I shouldn't. I turn towards Grady before getting in, "Grady. I-uh- I can't do this. I needed someone to help me forget my ex, and that he is coming to Dublin next week. And I thought it could be you." I waved my hand at him.

"Ah, makes sense."

"It makes sense, and I just don't know what to do. I didn't want to break up with my ex, but I did. And I regret it, but I lost myself, and I guess with this new job, I am finding myself and-"

"Sounds like a lot," Grady said, with eyes showing concern and care.

"It is," I said with a sigh.

"Well, it sounds like you need a friend more than a one-night stand. I'm happy to be an ear."

Looking up at Grady, I could tell he really meant that. I knew I had made my first real friend in Dublin.

13
emma

2 WEEKS BEFORE ST. *Patrick's Day…*

Hurrying along the sidewalk, I was heading to a GAA match: Dublin vs. Galway. I was meeting my new friend, Grady, at the game. Grady and I had exchanged numbers, and since the pub, we had seen each other a few times. Today was our first big outing outside of drinks and coffee. But honestly, he was becoming someone I really enjoyed having as a friend. Since moving to Dublin this would be my first official sport outing, and of course it would be to experience a soccer, nay, a football match, and I was excited. Any normal person would have experienced more events in Dublin their first year of moving here. But not this girl. No, I built up a wall of sadness, a few one-night stands to scratch the itch, and drowned myself in beer, whiskey, and work. But I was slowly feeling like myself again. Today would be the first day that I did something for fun with a new friend. The excitement I felt was most welcome.

As I approached, I saw Grady at the same time he saw me. He was waving, and he looked so happy. He was wearing a Dublin football scarf, and his cheeks were painted.

"Wow, Grady! You are quite the fan."

"Sure am. I love football. Now let's get inside. Today is going to be a great day." His enthusiasm was infectious. He gestured, and we went inside to the match.

Two hours later, my voice was hoarse from screaming and cheering. I had never had so much fun at a live sporting event. Being with Grady was also a blast. There was no pressure. Just him and the rest of the fans around us, having a great time watching the world's favorite sport. Being in the crowd, I swear I made about twenty new friends, became a soccer expert, and felt like I had played a full ninety-minute game.

"Want to get some food?" Grady asked afterwards.

"Definitely. I need food to sop up all the beer I drank." I giggled.

We walked for a while, talking about the game and cheering with other fans who were heading to pubs. It was nice just to feel normal and like I had no cares in the world. I had been stressed about St. Patrick's Day coming up and about Everett, Lola, and, most importantly, Joel coming. It had been stressing me out. But today, it was like the stress was all gone.

Honestly, since telling Piper about Joel, I felt like a weight had been lifted. But I knew I still needed to talk to Joel. I needed to tell him the full truth and that, well, I still loved him.

Sitting in a pub and ordering fish and chips, Grady sat at the bar and stared at me with a puzzled look, "What's on yer mind?"

"Nothing," I said.

"Something is. I can see it on your face. You smile, but then something flits across'd it, and I can see it makes you sad and worried. So spill."

"I don't know if I can just spill," I said.

"Sure ya can. It will probably help. Maybe ya need to move on from whatever is holding ya back."

"Maybe. I don't know."

"Do it. Just let it out. Take a breath and let it out."

Something told me I should let it out. That it would be easier the more I let things out and off my heart.

So I took a deep breath in, and when I let it out, I said in one breath, "IleftmysecretboyfriendbecauseIlostourbabyandmovedhere...ahhhhhh-hhhh." I exhaled.

Grady looked at me puzzled, "What was that?"

I smiled at him. "Sorry, it just all came out so fast. I said, "I left my secret boyfriend because I lost our baby and moved here."

Saying it a second time to Grady was even easier.

"Ah. Well, how do you feel now that you've said it?"

"Better. It was easier to say. I told my friend Piper a while back. She was the first and only person I told. Telling her took so much pressure off of me and took so much grief and sadness I had been carrying around off my back. But I think this time was easier. Maybe talking about it more and more makes it all easier."

"Probably." He said.

"My ex is coming here in two weeks for St. Patrick's Day. I haven't seen him since before I left New York, and I am really nervous."

"That's ter be expected."

"Yes, but I need to talk to him, tell him everything. And I think I need to let him know I still love him. Because I do. I miss him. Every time something happens, I want to text or call him right away. But I know I crushed him."

"Well, I think you should talk to him. It's never any good to keep it all in. Let it all out."

"Are you some wise man or something?" I asked jokingly.

"Nope. Just yer friend, who has been there. And I didn't get the chance to tell the woman I loved, that I still loved her."

"Oh. Why not?"

"She died while on the way to meet me so we could talk," Grady said. His eyes showed the deep sadness he still felt.

"Oh my gosh. I am so sorry, Grady. I had no idea." I leaned over and hugged him. He hugged me back.

"It's alright. That was years ago. But what I am trying to say is, don't hold it in. If you love the guy, let him know sooner rather than later. Don't build up your fear. Build up the love. You never know what could or will happen."

"You're right."

"I know I am." He said with a smile. It was so good to see a smile on his face after his revelation. His story and words made me realize he was truly right. I needed to let Joel know how I felt, tell him why I left. But it also made me realize that maybe the reason Grady was in my life as a friend was that I needed someone who understood.

"Grady, thank you for sharing your story with me. If you ever want to talk about her more, or talk, I am here."

"I know. Thank you. I am here for you, too. Now tell me more."

So I told him everything about the baby, the loss, and me leaving Joel and New York. I told him about how I needed to just grieve by myself and learn just to be a human again, and I didn't feel like I could do that if I stayed. I knew now I was running away and protecting myself, and protecting Joel. I was protecting us and our happy love story. I didn't want to tarnish it with this unimaginable loss and sadness. But now I knew I needed to let him in, and trust him, and our invisible string that bound us together as soulmates.

Dublin had helped me heal, and now I needed the courage to finish healing the things I had broken before leaving New York.

14
joel

2 DAYS BEFORE ST. Patrick's ...

Staring out the window of the jet, my dreadful nerves sank in deep. I knew this trip to Ireland was going to either bring Emma and me back together or seal our breakup. But honestly, there was no way in hell that Emma and I were done. I felt like a phony having to see her and pretend I was healed. But I wasn't. In reality, my feelings were all over the place, but more than anything, I needed to focus on winning her back, making her feel safe, and showing her she was it for me.

My travels showed me that more than anything, I needed to fight for her—for us.

As the plane flew towards Dublin, my game plan came into fruition. I'd take the next few days before heading to Emma's, checking on my family's company Dublin office and my new headquarters, then I'd make sure I could do everything in my power to show her why we were the endgame. We were it.

A year ago, when I wrote that letter, I had said goodbye and let her know she would always be the love of my life. But my time travelling around the world made me realize that the love she and I had was a permanent mark. It was love that stood the boundaries of time. Writing that letter, I was in a world of hurt but I still loved her more than anything. Now I had a new world perspective and still loved her more than anything.

France was the first stop on my globe-trotting adventure of healing. I ate my way through all the food, drank wine like it was my actual job, and I met some nice French women. But nothing I did got rid of my feelings and thoughts of Emma. We had an office in Paris, and so I did some work, but I think everyone knew I needed time off and time to reset.

After France, I went down to Sydney, where I rented a bungalow, surfed, and met some nice Aussie women. But more than anything, I went into the Outback; I volunteered with animal rescues, and also learned about the Great Barrier Reef. It was the first time my eyes opened up to what the world was going through and how I could do my small part in helping to make it better.

Then I went to Thailand, where I volunteered for three months solely at an Elephant sanctuary in Chiang Mai. Elephants were majestic creatures that taught me love, compassion, and resilience. My favorite elephant was Medo, who came to the sanctuary in 2006. If anything, her compassion, and demeanor taught me these things. After Thailand and a strong decision on whether I should stay or go, my mother convinced me to head to Germany and then Amsterdam to get back into work. My time at the sanctuary cleared my head and my heart, but maybe she was right, and I needed to get back into the swing of things.

Germany was picture perfect, I drank beer, enjoyed Oktoberfest, and had a great time. But I took time to travel in and out of the country, learning about WWI and WWII. The more I learned about history in other parts of the world and the more I worked with animals and people, the more I learned patience, kindness, and resolve. I started noticing that the more "mundane" things were precious and that the big or expensive things really had no meaning.

My final stop was Amsterdam to help secure leadership in that office for one of our companies. In my downtown, I thought I would be back to drinking or partying my sorrows away, but my travels had changed me. Instead, anyone could find me volunteering at a homeless shelter and working with underserved youth. Let me tell you, those kids taught me more about life than any adult ever could. One kid threw out compliments to everyone and oozed kindness. He taught me that it didn't cost a thing to compliment someone, and chances are it made that person smile and have a better day.

Now, on this plane, my travels and my education over the last year or so had me leaning into the fact that I needed to fight for Emma. Fighting for our love and showing her that we were inevitable—that we always had been, would be my number one prerogative while I was in Dublin. My second would be setting up the Dublin office to be my new headquarters.

A few hours later, the jet landed, and I rode in the town car to what would be my hotel for a few nights before I stayed at Emma's. Her brother had told me he had secured lodging for me in her other guestroom, and I had to take the chance to be in proximity to her.

In the hotel room, I quickly had my stuff dropped off and called my assistant to make sure the office was ready for me to head in. She gave me the go-ahead, so my driver took me there.

Walking into the rustic building, a calming and contented sense washed over me, letting me know that this was where I was meant to be. To win my girl back, I needed to be right here in Dublin, make sure my new HQ would help my family's company and me succeed. Because I would be here forever, either winning Emma back or living here with her for however long she wanted.

I would wait, I would work hard for her and show her that we no longer could fight the darkness of being apart. I needed to revive this relationship from the dead and show Emma that our souls were tied together. This love was everything.

Sitting at my new walnut desk, I had a flashback to telling her how much we were permanent and tattooed on each other's hearts.

It was her birthday party. Emma had just turned twenty-one, and I watched her blow out her birthday candles on the cake that her college best friend, Stasia, had bought her. After blowing out her candles, she shot her hands into the air and smiled. I swear she made all the lights in the dimly lit restaurant flicker to fluorescent with that gorgeous full-toothed smile. Sitting across from her at this table for twenty, I was just glad to have been invited by her, but if you asked her brother, I was invited by him because he had no idea that his sister and I had been in each other's romantic orbit for a few years now.

After looking at the whole table and saying thank you, her gaze finally landed on me. Her gaze pierced me, even if no one else knew what was going on between us. She gave me a smirk, and I felt it resonate throughout my body, knowing what it meant. It meant, thank you, I'm glad you're here, unwrap me later ...

Later on in the evening, we were at a club in Soho, and she wanted to dance. She pushed her buzzed self between her brother and me while we were at the bar and said, "You, you will be dancing with me right now! It's my birthday."

How could I say no?

We could dance in front of everyone, and they would think it was just us as friends. But I was relishing feeling her hips pushing into mine and her hands clasped behind my neck. My hands grasped slightly above her hips tightly. I stared down at her, and then I told her, "Can we make this real? Your soul and mine are intertwined. We are tattooed on each other's hearts. Say yes to being mine ... please."

She pulled away slightly and showed me that toothy grin. Her emerald eyes sparkled with the affirmation that what I felt was what she felt. She leaned to speak into my ear, "Yes." All of a sudden, it was like we were floating in the air while we danced to more songs, and I was allowed to grind her in public.

15
emma

1 DAY BEFORE ST. *Patrick's Day ...*

One day. Just one fucking day left before Joel ended up in this guestroom that had become a dumping ground for all the boxes I didn't want to open and other junk. I had been working my way through it all and unboxing and organizing, but this process made me realize I had way too much stuff. I ended up having a huge donation pile and reused a good amount of the boxes for donations. Blaring Taylor Swift's song, "Don't Blame Me", to maximum volume as I worked my way through the final two boxes. Opening the second to last one, A note written in distinct handwriting sat perfectly encased on the top. This was a box that Joel had sent, and one would think the letter on top would have crumpled or slipped, but no. The cross-Atlantic trip didn't jostle or rumple it. There the letter sat. Taunting me. My name was written on it, glaring at me as if I didn't pick it up soon, it was going to curse me or something. Hands trembling, I reached into the box to grab the envelope. I held it up, contemplating whether I should finish a bottle of wine before reading.

"Hellooooo...Emma?" A familiar female voice said.

"Helloooooooo?" I whirled and put the letter in my back pocket, heading to the door and walked slowly down the hallway of my cottage. A familiar face popped up at the top of the stairs, and all of a sudden, I felt like I could cry. There was Lola in all of her whimsical glory, smiling at me like we hadn't seen each other in months, because we hadn't. Seeing her, I didn't realize how much I needed just to have one of my best friends near. I immediately grasped her and held her tightly with tears starting to well up in my eyes.

"Hey Em. I've missed you. Tell me everything." Lola said.

Not letting go, my tears started flowing.

"Hey, hey, shhhhh. What's goin' on?" She asked.

"I-I- I can't yet. But soon, I will tell you." Pulling away, I asked, "Where is Ev?"

"He was helping the driver unload the luggage. Tell me what has got you down?" She wiped a tear off my cheek.

"I need to come clean, but I don't think I can do it in front of Everett yet. But I think I need you to sit with me while I read something."

"Emma!" I heard a loud yell.

Bounding up the steps with a small travel bag, Everett stopped in his tracks as he looked back and forth between Lola and me.

"Are you just that happy to see us, Em?" He chuckled lightly, coming over to hug me.

"Yeah. I missed you guys a lot." Lying to him.

"Well, as much as I would never admit it in public, I missed you a lot, too. Hence why we will be buying a place here and also staying for a few weeks."

"Sorry, Em. I told him we should rent a house, but he insisted we stay with you because he missed you." Lola said apologetically.

"Oh, it is no problem. I am so happy you're here. Anyway, you know where your room is. Are there more bags?" I asked.

"Tons, but Grady said he would bring them in, and then I will bring them up to our room."

"Grady? Who is Grady?" I asked, wondering how weird it was that I knew a Grady.

"Oh yeah, he is the driver I hired for the time we are here. I could have rented a car, but I will be working on some things, and with us looking at places and going to see the sights, I thought it would just be easier to have a driver."

"So Grady will be hanging out with us for the next few weeks?" I asked.

"Yup. He is downstairs if you want to go introduce yourself."

"Sure, I'll ask if he needs any water or anything." I went down the stairs, and Lola followed. My brother's heavy footfall could be heard going down the upstairs hallway to their room. As I hit the bottom landing, the door was open, and I saw the man coming up to the stoop with two large rolling suitcases.

Most people say they would have stopped dead in their tracks at the sight of the man, but they didn't. Instead, I kept walking towards him and said, "Well, well, if it isn't my new bestie?"

"Emma! Is this? Is this your place?"

"It sure is." I smiled and hugged Grady.

"Wow, fate must really be pushing us together. I didn't realize that your brother was talking about you. Emma is a pretty common name for Americans, ya know." He smiled flirtatiously and jokingly.

"That is true." I said, "So it looks like we will be together a lot over the next few weeks."

"Sounds like it."

"Well, it sounds fun. Do you want water or whiskey? Beer? I see my brother has you doing all this hard work."

"Ah, yes, water is good."

Grady followed me to the kitchen and stood at my kitchen island. I went and grabbed a glass, going to my fridge to pour him a glass of water.

"This place is nice. Great view." He said, pointing out towards the sea.

"It is. I fell in love with it. It brings me a lot of peace."

"Has it brought you peace?"

Looking at him, I could tell he was curious. Again, I had the feeling I could trust him like he was a genuine friend. "Kind of. I needed something that would soothe my soul. This place popped up, and I could feel it calling to me. The view, the homey vibe—this place definitely heals. But as you know, it will take more to heal me."

"Well at least the cottage helps."

We both stared out the window while he sipped his water. The next thing we knew, my brother was barging into the kitchen mumbling.

"What's crawled up your butt, Everett?" I asked.

"Work." He said. Then he stopped, staring at both Grady and me. "Do you two know each other?"

"Kind of. He is my friend." I said.

"We met at a pub and became fast friends," Grady said, smiling down at me as if we had an inside joke.

"Oh," Everett said, and he looked like he was mad ... confused ... maybe about to shit himself.

"Are you okay, Ev?"

"Uh, yeah. I need to make a quick call. Um. Is there good service by the cliffs?" He was being shady all of a sudden, and it had my hackles raised.

"Yes? But you get good service in here, too."

"Yeah, but I need some air and privacy." He was sharp.

"Okay," I said standoffishly. "Fine. Grady, have a nice day." I don't know what it was, but Everett being rude just pissed me off, and I needed to get out of the kitchen. I walked off before Grady could say bye, or my brother could exit. I was just pissed, but also, deep down, my nerves were at a level ten, and I was not ready to see Joel. So everything was going to irk me until we got the initial hello between each other over with.

After my talk with Piper a few months ago, I knew that I needed to come clean to Joel. But now that it was in the last moments before seeing him, I didn't know if I dared to do it. And honestly, I didn't know how he felt about me. I hoped I hadn't done so much damage that he hated me. But then I second-guess myself, thinking that if he hated me, he wouldn't be staying at my house and spending St. Patrick's with me.

It was an emotional and scary roller coaster ride I was on right now, and I couldn't wait for tomorrow, but I also couldn't wait for it never to come. It was a very raw mixture of feelings. I sat in my room and grabbed a book, thinking it might help take my mind off things, but instead my mind kept wandering to thoughts of Joel. More than that, it kept drifting towards the happy and loving moments with Joel.

The moments when he held me in bed and kissed the top of my head while we watched a movie. Or how he always sang to Creedence Clearwater Revival in the shower. Then there was the moment he told me he loved me for the first time. Or that very first time we kissed in my family's guest house. These happy thoughts made me realize that everything would be ok.

I touched the triskele pendant I found on my windowsill. I had put it on a gold chain and wore it religiously along with my Claddagh ring. They made me feel lucky and protected. And that whatever was coming my way would be amazing. Touching my pendant, I suddenly felt the urge to go to the guest room I had labeled, "Joel's Room."

Opening the door slowly and wandering in, I immediately saw the envelope Joel had written to me, and my heart lurched. My stomach had butterflies, because something told me it wouldn't be a sad note.

Reaching for it and finally opening it, I sat on the edge of the bed, which I had bought specifically with him in mind. He loved a very firm mattress, and I knew this one would be perfect for him.

Taking the deepest of breaths, I read it.

My hands shook relentlessly as I unfolded the letter.

My name, Emma, was written in his familiar, sharp handwriting. His embossed initials were atop the stationery.

Emma,

I'm writing this because I don't know what else to do. I'm sitting in my apartment, staring at the last box of your things. I almost sent it off unopened, but thank God, or fate, or divine intervention, I didn't.

I found it, Em. The little cedar box with the triskeles. Your Irish memory box.

Inside were a positive pregnancy test and a photo of an embryo, time-stamped right after Piper and Lane's wedding. Nine weeks.

I know.

My world has tilted on its axis. Everything makes a dark, horrible kind of sense now, but it doesn't make the questions any less deafening.

Why?

Why didn't you tell me? After all these years of hiding, after finally getting to a place where we were a we, why would you keep something this monumental—this life-altering—a secret? Why did you carry a truth this immense, this beautiful, and this devastating all by yourself?

You left me, Emma. You dumped me for a job, and blocked me. You let me think I was just some guy you could walk away from and bounce back from quickly, like every other breakup. You let me play the angry, broken man at Walla's, and you sat there with a secret this enormous and life-altering.

I truly thought you left because you stopped believing in us. But now I see you thought you were protecting me, protecting both of us. I know you. And you did this because you love me, and you also needed to heal. You needed to heal in your own way. You're hurting and grieving. And I'm so sorry. No one deserves to feel the loss you have gone through.

Even though I started this letter with questions, I am also writing out my feelings as they come, and well, I want you to know that even though I want to know why I couldn't be the one to hold you and grieve with you, I also am glad you are doing what you need to do to grieve. To heal. To relearn how to love...

I'm sending you this box, but I need you to know I love you, Emma. I have loved you since you were a ten-year-old in a red polka-dot bikini who told me she was going to marry me. You are my person: my soul, my heart.

The despair I'm feeling is unbearable. You were going to be a mother. I was going to be a father. And now, all I have is a photo of a life we almost had, and a crushing sense of loss. The choice you made and the secret you kept doesn't change the love I have for you.

I'm leaving for France tomorrow to put some distance between myself and this intense pain, but I can't leave without sending this to you. I need you to know that I know. And I need you to know that I still love you. I will always love you. I will be here waiting with open arms to love you again when you're ready.

Forever yours,

J

16
joel

ST. *Patrick's Day ...*

Today was the first time I would see Emma since getting drinks at Walla's over a year ago. I was nervous as hell, but I had been here a few days and was working on making sure I had all the tools and tricks up my sleeve to win her back. And if I didn't win her back during this trip, I was staying in Dublin indefinitely to let her know I would love her forever. The stakes felt impossibly high.

My driver pulled up to Emma's cottage, and bricks hit the bottom of my stomach. I was nervous as hell, and I just hoped this went smoothly. Getting out of the car, I slowly strode up to the door. I looked down and halted. In between the cobblestone walkway, a four-leaf clover poked through. Bending to grab it, I couldn't believe my luck. Maybe this would all turn out okay. Standing back up, I knocked on the door and waited.

Hearing footsteps from the inside, the door swung open, and I held my breath.

"Hey, man!" Everett said, reaching out to pull me into a hug.

"Hey, bud," I said, smiling when I saw my best friend.

"Joely Roley Poley!" Lola yelled, pushing her way past Everett to come and hug me as well. Her hug was comforting, and I was grateful that these two opened the door and helped to calm me down.

Looking up, I thought I would see Emma, but she wasn't around.

"Where is Emma?" I asked.

Everett and Lola looked at each other, then looked at me. "She went to the store. She said she needed to stock up on her wine and Macallan for you." Lola said.

"I think she was just getting some liquid courage in her before you came," Everett said not mincing words.

"I probably should have done the same," I said. Knowing that Lola probably knew the entire story either from Emma or Everett. Or even Piper.

"Why do you get settled? Emma made up a whole room for you here on the main floor. It is really nice," Lola said while she walked towards a hallway.

"Sounds good." I followed her to what would be my room, and when I went through the door, I could have gasped like a lady in fucking waiting. Emma had meticulously picked out the furniture, and it was all stuff I would have picked out for myself.

"She keeps calling this 'Joel's Room,' so I am pretty sure that no one else can stay in it." Lola had a smirk and a knowing glint in her eyes.

"It's amazing." I was floored and couldn't get the words out. "Where is Emma's room?"

"Right next to yours." She said.

I held up the four-leaf clover, "I found this outside. I thought they weren't real, but a few days ago I found out they are really rare and occur because of a mutation in the three-leaf clover. But they symbolize faith, hope, love, and luck. I picked it, and I am hoping it gives Emma and me all of those things."

Lola had tears welling up in her eyes, "That's really sweet, Joel. You two are going to make it. I have hope, love, and faith for both of you." She patted my shoulder and left me in my room. Standing there, I took in all the little details Emma put into the room then I left. Every cushion, every piece of wood—it all felt like a confession of her love for me.

I went straight into Emma's room and put the four-leaf clover on her pillow. I looked around and saw a small wooden desk. Walking over, I wrote a quick note, set it by the clover, and went back to my room to unpack.

The waiting was agonizing. A few hours later, I heard a car door and knew Emma must have made it back home. I had been patiently waiting with Everett and Lola. It was nice to catch up with both of them and let loose. They asked more questions about my plans, and I told them I was here to stay and that I would be fighting tooth and nail for Emma. When she finally came through the door, Emma slowly walked in with a wobble in her step. Seeing her, I knew instantly she had probably gone too far with her liquid courage. Also, it was St. Patty's, so it was probably hard to say no to all the beverages.

Slurring, Emma said, "Luuuuushee, I'm home!!!!!" in a Ricky Ricardo voice.

"Emma. It's 11 am. How are you already this toasted? We are supposed to go to lunch soon." Everett said in a worried and angry voice.

"Shup, Ev. I went for breaky and had a few green drinks. And now I'm here. I need a nap and here." She thrust a bag at Everett. It clanked, letting us know there were more bottles of booze.

"Joel is here, Emma. Get it together." Everett said more sternly.

"Joel." She looked at me and sobered for an instant, "My Joely. Can you tuck me in?" She came over, arms spread wide, and hugged me. It wasn't the reception I wasn't expecting or necessarily hoping for. But it would do. I would take a hug over anger or a cold shoulder any day.

"Hey there, Em. Let's get you to bed. We can nap."

"Okay. Take me away, cowboy."

"Cowboy?" Lola whispered to Everett.

"She gets all Shania Twain on us when she's drunk, remember," Everett whispered back.

I lifted Emma and carried her bride-style to her room, laying her down on her bed. I pushed her hair back from her face.

"I missed you. I'm sorry." She slurred.

"It's okay. I'm here." I kissed her forehead and looked back at her. She had fallen fast asleep. Emma looked beautiful, serene, and worry-free when she slept. I used to love watching her sleep. It was creepy, but I just loved how relaxed and innocent she was. Like nothing could weigh her down.

Walking out, I went back to Everett and Lola, "Well, she is passed out. Let's give her until 12:30 or one, and she should be good."

"She must have been really nervous to see you," Lola said.

"Well, we were both nervous. But now I bet Em will be embarrassed. So I might need to reassess my approach. Ya know, factor this in and make sure she knows that nothing she does is embarrassing."

"You really love her," Everett said.

"Yeah, Ev. I really do."

Leaving them, I went outside, and a man was standing in the driveway. "Um ... hello."

"Hiya. You need a ride?" He asked in his Irish lilt.

"Um, yeah. I think I do. I wanted to get something for Emma. A hostess gift."

"Ah, yes. Our dear Emma. She would like that."

"Are you friends with Emma?" I asked, not masking my jealousy.

"You could say that." He said with a smirk almost like he was egging me on.

"How?" I said deadpan.

"She picked me up at the pub." He said.

It felt as if the ground beneath me gave way. I felt like I was falling. Here I was about to do something for Emma while she slept, and I was meeting a fuckbuddy of hers? This was going to make it harder for me to win her back. So much harder.

"Oh."

"Yeah. She's a good one. So, where we headed?" He asked.

"Um... I think I'll just stay here until Emma wakes up. What's your name?"

"Grady. Everett hired me to be the driver while he is here."

"Ah. Well, thanks, man." I said and turned on my heel to head back into the house. I went looking for Lola immediately. I found her in the sunroom, "Lola, who is Grady, and is he dating Emma?"

"What? Grady?" Lola said, confused.

"Grady. The driver. Is he and Emma together?"

Interrupted, Everett said, "No. They are not together. They are just friends."

"Are you sure?"

"Yes. Positive. I overheard their conversation in the kitchen." Everett said.

"Alright. Thanks, Ev." I paced, my relief short-lived. "So Emma has been with other men?"

"I mean, you've been with other women, right?" Lola said.

"Yes. I just need to know if I have any competition."

"You don't have any competition. Honestly, with how Emma showed up this morning, I don't think anyone holds a candle to how she feels about you." Lola swayed up to me and hugged me. She pulled away, "Joel, you're it for her. You're hers, and she is yours. That's it. End of story."

"You sure?" I had so many doubts.

"Positive."

"I think I am going to take a walk. I'll wake Emma. I think she and I need to talk one-on-one."

"Can do," Everett said.

"Thanks, guys."

Walking out the back door, I went towards the cliffs to walk along the coastline. The sea roared, and the wind was gentle. It felt like I was in the right spot and everything was going to work out. I just needed Emma to wake up, sober up, and do everything in my manly power to make her mine again. I don't have a script or a plan anymore for getting her back. I just have my truth. Feeling content after a long walk, I walked back along the green path that butts up against the coastline. A sense of certainty settled in my gut. Deep down, I know everything will work out.

Once I get back to Emma's house, I can only hope that Emma is awake. I sigh before entering her cottage. When I walk in, I see her. Her long brunette hair, her perfect curves, and those deep emerald eyes. Seeing her, the big breath I took leaves my body because she takes my breath away.

"Hell, Emma," I say.

"Hey, Joel. I've missed you."

17
emma

ST. *Patrick's Day Morning ...*

I woke up that morning, and I knew I needed to get my head on right before Joel entered my Cottage. Hoping our first meeting in over a year would go well, I just needed a breather from Lola and Everett. They kept hovering like I was some fragile porcelain doll. It was annoying.

So I woke up, put on black leggings, my tennis shoes, a long-sleeve white shirt, and a green vest since it was St. Patrick's Day. I braided my hair into two pigtail braids, put on a NY green ball cap, and had Grady drive me downtown, where I was just going to pop into a little store and get some booze for later. But instead, I got swept up in the festivities. Let me roll that back. I didn't just get swept up; I plunged headfirst.

When I say swept up, I mean I got swept up into the full-on parade happening. Shots suddenly started being poured down my throat. I ended up at a random pub where I took part in a green beer drinking contest, and I even danced to several pub songs.

By the time Grady found me, I was three sheets to the wind and ready to see Joel.

"Emma, you're drunk and we need to get you home so you can enjoy tonight."

"I'm definitely going to enjoy tonight because I'm going to climb Joel like a tree."

That was the last thing I remembered.

What I can only assume was five hours, or maybe only ten minutes, later, I vaguely remembered seeing a blurry Joel, calling him 'cowboy', and getting into my bed.

Later that afternoon ...

Cotton was coating the inside of my mouth. I knew I had been snoring since my mouth tasted and felt like straight ass. I tried turning over, but I could still feel the weird, sloshy feeling of being drunk. I was more sober, but definitely still slightly buzzed. Once I opened my eyes fully, I realized there was a four-leaf clover lying on the pillow next to me with a note.

Emma,

Found this and thought of you. Maybe some luck will be headed our way today. Just wanted to let you know I was thinking of you and I really, really missed you.

XO, J

He missed me. He left me a note— a simple note, saying that he missed me. My heart started thumping like Thumper from Bambi. Maybe he still loved me, and all hope was not lost. I read the note over and over—memorizing every last word. I then spun the four-leaf clover between my thumb and pointer finger, back and forth, back and forth, staring at it as the mid-day sun hit just right in my room.

I missed him, too. So much. And I needed to work through all the bullshit, have a conversation with him, and hopefully move on... with him.

Popping up out of my bed, I went to my bathroom to freshen up. I did my hair, brushed my teeth, redid a little bit of my makeup, and brushed my hair out before putting my NY cap back on.

Taking a deep breath of courage, I walked out to my kitchen... slightly wobbly from my morning shenanigans but still confident nonetheless. I walk out and see Lola and Ev. Then the door opens, and in walks Joel.

He is more muscular and tanner. His brown hair is lighter from the sun, as if he has spent more time outside. His eyes are a deeper, darker shade of green and hold an ease in them that I never saw before. It's like he lived a whole other life, and it changed him into a softer man.

"Hello Emma." He says.

Deciding to lay it all bare, I say, "Hey, Joel. I've missed you." I saunter over to him slowly, a bit nervously, and a little scared, but I hug him. Tight. He wraps his large, muscular arms around me, and I deflate for the first time in over a year. It's like all of the stress, pain, sadness, and loss, evaporate with that one hug from Joel. It makes me realize that I was wrong. I shouldn't have protected him or our love story. Instead, I should have leaned in and had these big arms and a full heart wrapping me in love to help through the grief and loss.

I pull Joel in tighter; I can't help it. I need this like I need air, food, and water. His touch, his heartbeat against mine, soothes me as nothing else can. I pull away and look up at him, still holding on to him though, "I really did miss you."

"Same. It's been too long or maybe the right amount of time." He speaks like a prophet. But I know what he means. Maybe it was too long to be separated. Or maybe it is what we needed. Who knows. What matters is that we are here together right now.

The day melted into evening. Several hours later, we are at a pub with karaoke. I took it easy so I could make sure I was in good enough shape to talk to Joel. He seemed to be doing the same. I noticed how much more water he drank than the green beer or whiskey. The night had been fun and like old times. We pub-hopped, played games, and had a great time. Everett and Lola were tanked and all over each other. Lola kept telling me how much I needed to be the first one to make a move on Joel and that she knew everything. I loved tipsy Lola, but I didn't need her telling me what to do to win back Joel.

As the night wore on, Joel and I grew friendlier and more touchier and in tune. It was like nothing had happened over the past year of being part of it. Maybe it was the booze, maybe it was that we both never stopped loving each other. Either way, it felt right. After getting my water topped off, Lola was screaming my name. I looked over at her, as she pointed up to the stage. Joel was standing there, mic in hand. His gaze was locked with mine. Those green eyes shone with a bit of unease, but also a lot of love. I smiled at him to let him know I saw him.

"Emma, this one is for you."

The music started, and the guitar melody took me back to when I was in my early twenties, Joel singing me this very song. It has an entirely different meaning now.

Joel sang with passion in his voice,

"Honey, you are a rock,
Upon which I stand
And I come here to talk
I hope you understand."

My heart fluttered, swelled, and leapt. Eyes welling deep with tears, I smiled at him and put my hands over my heart.

"The green eyes
Yeah, the spotlight
Shines upon you
And how could
Does anybody deny you?
I came here with a load
And it feels so much lighter now I met you
And honey, you should know

That I could never go on without you
Green eyes."

Then Joel walks towards me, still singing on the black mic, and sings right in front of me. Looking down and literally singing his heart out.

He ends the song, with his hand taking one of mine, and sings the last few words, "*Honey, you are a rock, upon which I stand.*"

And I lose it. The dam broke and tears overflowed, rushing down my cheeks. I wrap my arms around him, and I kiss him like I would die if we didn't kiss right at that very moment.

"I'm so sorry. So sorry. Please forgive me." I sob out through my tears.

"It's okay, Em. I love you. Still. And always." He kisses me back and then pulls away to wipe away my tears.

"FUCK YES! Next round is on me!" I hear Everett yell to the crowded pub, and cheers erupt. Joel and I ignore it and continue to kiss, hold each other, and cry.

18
joel

SHORTLY AFTER MY song and kissing the shit out of Emma, I leaned down and whispered in her ear if we could head to her house because I wanted to be with just her. Only her. We needed to talk. She shook her head in silent agreement, grabbed my hand, and led me out of the pub. I texted Everett and Lola to let them know we would order a taxi back to the house. Lola replied immediately, letting me know they would have Grady drive them back soon.

Once Emma and I got back to her place, she led me into the sunroom, where we settled onto her white sofa, facing each other but close. It was like we were back to when I was twenty and she was nineteen, sitting on the couch in her parent's pool house, and me spilling out that I liked her. I laid my arm along the back of the couch and reached for her hand. My fingers intertwined with hers. I wanted to touch her as we talked. I needed constant contact to ground us, to let her know that I wasn't going anywhere.

"Joel. I am so sorry." She said with fresh tears falling.

Leaning over to wipe them away, I said, "Emma, I get why you did it. I understand why you left me. I am just sorry that you thought you had to carry this all by yourself. That was never supposed to be yours alone, Emma. Nothing you could have done or said would have broken me or us. Nothing. I love you."

Letting out a shaky breath, Emma looked at our hands joined on the back of the couch. She rubbed her thumb back and forth on my hand.

"I know that now. But I thought I was protecting you and, well, our happy love story. I didn't think it would break you. But I thought it would change you and thus change us. When I lost the baby, it was like all my happy dreams just completely shattered. I had this picture of us in my head, and that image was ripped to shreds. It was broken. It was just so much emotion and hurt all at once, and it was unbearable."

Emma," I said so empathetically, "I get it. I really do. It all makes sense to me." I scooted closer and tipped her chin to look directly at me. Her eyes were a sea green with a red tinge from the crying. The tears made them seem like an endless sea. Looking at her, all I saw was my best friend, the love of my life, and the most beautiful girl I had ever seen in this entire world.

"It makes sense because you have been spending over nine years keeping us a secret, and somewhere in that time, you stopped letting yourself lean on me the way you should have been able to." I paused. "That one is partly on me, too."

"It's not-"

"It is, Em." I paused to gather my thoughts. "I let the fear of losing your brother's friendship get in the way of us. If I had fought harder and sooner, maybe you wouldn't have been at the doctor's, going through all of this alone." Tears started to fall down my cheeks now.

She grabbed my face with both hands. "I should have called you. I knew I messed up. I should have called you the first time I realized that the only person I wanted to talk to was you."

"You should have."

"I felt so much joy when I found out. I couldn't wait to tell you. I thought everything was perfect and going according to fate. And then it didn't."

Right then, I pulled Emma onto my lap, and she lay her head on my chest. "I was happy for about thirty seconds after I opened the box and realized what I saw. The sonogram photo ... then I realized what it all meant, and I was thoroughly crushed. Anyway, I just want you to know that you don't have to carry all of this alone. You never have to carry anything alone."

"I'm sorry I ran to Dublin. I robbed you of the chance to make a choice with me. I just ended things and ran."

"I know, but maybe it was the right path for us. I learned a lot in my time away, and eventually, we can discuss it all. But right now, I need you to know and hear me when I say that I am not here to feel sorry for you or for me. I am not here to get closure or because of any obligations. I am here because I love you. Fuck do I love you. I moved my office here so I could permanently be here with you. You are where I want to be and where I need to be. That's it. And if you're not ready for me to be here just quite yet, I will give you that space. But I will be here waiting until you're ready."

"You moved your headquarters here?" She asked, her voice barely above a whisper.

"Yup. Well, at least my office. HQ is still in New York, but I will be working from wherever you are. Even if that means I am in Dublin. I'm staying."

She stared at me. A slow, incredulous smile spread across her face. "I mean, my mother thought it was romantic. Your brother cried when he heard what I did. Lola told me I was doing the right thing. And Piper and Lane were fully on board."

"You really moved here for me." She said matter-of-factly.

"I did."

"And Everett cried?"

"He did. It was very masculine and dignified."

"Sure..." she chuckled.

She had a smile that stayed on her face, and I basked in its glow. We sat there in silence, taking it all in.

"What do we do now, Joel?"

"Whatever we want. We can take this day by day. Or go at lightning speed. I am at your whim."

Emma thought, twirling the triskele necklace at her throat.

"I have been finding things, signs. I found this Claddagh ring with a Ruby. It symbolizes loyalty, friendship, and love. If you wear it on your right hand with the heart facing out, you're single. If the heart is facing inward, it means you're taken. If you move it to your left hand with the heart out, it means you're engaged. And if it is on your right hand with the heart pointed inward, it means you're married."

Nodding, I watched her as she moved the ring on her left hand from outward to inward. Indicating she was now taken. It was a silent, profound declaration. She was taken, and I was the one who took her. I smiled, and my eyes watered again.

"I also found this triskele necklace in the house. It means life, death, and rebirth. It also could mean past, present, and future. Everything I have found lately seems to be leaving me little clues. And I think it is pointing me in the direction that you are my loyal best friend and lover. You are my past, my present, and my future."

I nodded more, too choked up for words.

"Joel." She said.

"Yeah."

"I love you."

We leaned our heads together, "I know, Em. I have loved you too since you were ten, in a red polka-dot bikini. Telling me you were going to marry me someday."

She blushed and pulled back.

"This is going to sound crazy, but you're my person, and I am yours. And well, maybe we should just cut the bullshit and get married."

"Get married?"

"Yes. I don't think we should start over. I want to move on to our future. So, Joel, will you marry me? Tonight? Tomorrow? Soon? I know it's crazy and we just apologized but-"

I didn't let her finish. I slammed my mouth to hers. "Yes, Em." Between kisses, I kept saying yes. Then I asked, "Would you really marry me tonight?"

"If we can find an officiant." She grinned, a brilliant, wild flash of Emma. And it was like fate was on our side cheering, because Everett and Lola screamed as they burst through the front door of the house. We approached them in the foyer, holding hands, and said, "We're getting married!" at the same time.

Drunk Everett and Lola smiled and clapped.

"But we need to find an officiant, now!" Emma said.

Grady emerged from behind Everett and Lola, a calm anchor in the chaos. "I could be of assistance. I am a registered officiant here in Dublin."

"You are? What?" Emma screamed, the question part disbelief, part pure joy.

"Yup. Sure am." Grady said with a knowing smile.

Emma and I looked at each other and smiled. Apparently Irish luck was finally, and irrevocably, on our side.

19
joel

THE NEXT MORNING…

We woke up the next morning, and I looked down to see Emma's hand resting on my chest. Her Claddagh ring was on her left hand, turned inward, showing she was married. With a lot of finagling, we were able to get everything done by 11:30 AM last night. Emma stirs, and I look to see green. All I see is her beautiful green eyes echoing love and happiness.

"Mornin'." I kiss her forehead.

She stretches slowly, "Mmmmmm … good morning, hubby."

"I like the sound of that wife."

"Are we actually married, though?" She asked.

Panic rose in me.

"I mean, I know we are married. But is it legal? We don't have the proper paperwork."

"I say it's legal. And we can figure out the paperwork later. I will text my lawyers to get it figured out stat." I kissed her again.

"I'm really happy."

"Me too, Em. Me too." I rolled her over onto her back and lay slightly on top. I kissed her mouth and then slowly and lightly kissed down her jaw and neck.

"I could wake up like this every morning." She moaned out.

"Good thing we can do this every morning now that we're married."

A little while later, Emma and I headed downstairs. Sitting at the kitchen island, Everett and Lola looked horribly hungover. Lola was wearing sweats, sunglasses, and her hair was a mess. Everett was also in sweats, and groaning, his face in his palms.

"Did you two get hit by a bus? You both look like shit." Then Emma laughed really loudly.

Both winced.

"Haha, Em. You know how crazy last night was. I barely remember all of us getting home." Everett said.

"Yeah, and I weirdly dreamt you two got married in the dark by the coastline." Lola groaned.

"We did get married on the coastline," I said.

"Grady married us. You two were there and sobbing." Emma said.

They both looked at us like we were nuts.

"Very funny," Everett said.

"It's true." Emma held up her ring hand. "Ask Grady, Ev. If you don't believe me."

Everett grabbed his phone off the countertop and called Grady. Grady answered fast, and Everett asked him if he had married Emma and me. Grady must have confirmed, because he just hung up.

"You have to call our parents. And Piper and Lane. Like now. I can't believe I missed it. I mean, I can't remember it. You two are really married?"

"We are."

Emma's phone started to ring. She looked at it and said, "Speaking of Piper. She is Facetiming me." Emma answered. "Hey, Pipes! How ya doin? Why are you up so early? Isn't it like five in the morning there?

"It is five. But we had a long night. Show me the whole group. Is everyone up? I am sure yesterday was crazy."

"It was, but we are all up," Emma said, and we moved to be behind Lola and Everett.

Next thing we knew, Piper was showing us she was in a hotel room, and Lane popped into the video holding a baby. We all yelled and said Congrats.

"He was born at 11:57 on St. Patrick's Day. We decided to name him Auley. A good Irish name." Lane said.

We all got a great view of Auley, the newest member of our little crew. I looked over at Emma to see if she was ok. If everything had worked out, we would already have had a baby. She looked back at me and nodded. Showing me that she was okay.

"Not to steal your thunder, but we have news too," Emma said.

She held up her ring finger, "Joel and I made up. And we just said, fuck it. Let's get married. So we did. Last night."

It was Piper and Lane's turn to scream.

After that, we continued talking until we could tell Piper was tired, and we said our goodbyes.

"Are you two going to do anything back home in Pine Hills?" asked Lola.

"We should," I said.

"Yeah, maybe this summer. I think that would be really good. But maybe we can do something in a few weeks with just Piper, Lane, and our parents to celebrate. Something intimate and family only."

I kissed the top of her head and said, "That sounds great, Em."

"Ew, . is this what I really have to get used to now?" Everett chimed in.

Lola elbowed him, "Stop being a dick."

20
emma

PIPER WAS SHOWING us she was in a hospital room, and Lane popped into the video holding a baby. We all yelled and said congrats, and I meant every word of it. I truly did. But the second I saw that tiny, perfect, brand new face on the screen, something happened in my chest that I was not entirely prepared for.

It was not sadness exactly. It was something more complicated than sadness. Something that sat right alongside joy and held its hand.

"He was born at 11:57 on St. Patrick's Day," Lane said, glowing in that specific way that new fathers glowed. It was like Lane had just witnessed something so enormous it had rearranged them from the inside out. "We decided to name him Auley. A good Irish name."

"Auley," I whispered to myself and smiled.

And he was. He really was. Round-cheeked and scrunchy-faced and wrapped up in one of those hospital blankets with the little stripes, blinking at the world like he was still deciding what to make of it. Piper was looking at him from behind the camera with an expression I had never seen on her face before. It was something so open, pure, and unguarded that it made my throat ache.

I felt Joel's hand find the small of my back.

It was barely anything. Just his hand, warm and steady, resting there like he was saying “I am right here” without saying a single word. I did not look at him right away. I kept my eyes on the screen, and smiled because I was genuinely happy. I was genuinely happy for them.

If everything had gone differently, we would have had a baby already.Not Auley's age. Younger. But already here. Already in the world. Already ours.

I had not let myself think about that in a while. I had gotten good at steering around it, avoiding it. But seeing Lane hold his son at five in the morning with that look on his face, and Piper looking like the moon was finally hung up in the sky, I could not steer around it fast enough.

I looked up at Joel.

He was already looking at me. Of course he was.

His expression was careful and soft and completely unguarded in the way that Joel's face rarely was with other people, but had always been with me. He was not trying to fix it, talk me out of it, or tell me, with his eyes, that I should not be feeling what I was feeling. He was just there. Feeling all of it, too. Acknowledging it quietly between us, the way only two people who had shared a loss could do across a crowded room, I nodded.

It was the smallest thing. Just one nod that said I'm okay, and also I'm not entirely okay, and also both of those things are true at the same time, and I think that is just how this is going to feel for a while.

He nodded back. His hand pressed a little more firmly against my back.“I know,” his hand said. “Me too.”

I turned back to the screen.

"Not to steal your thunder," I said, and my voice came out steadier than I expected, "but we have news too."

I held up my ring finger.

"Joel and I made up. And we just said, fuck it. Let's get married. So we did. Last night."

The screaming from Piper and Lane was loud enough that Auley startled in his father's arms, and Lane had to do the instinctive new-dad bounce to settle him. Everett winced. Lola burst into tears for what I was fairly certain was the third time in twelve hours.

And Joel laughed low and warm and completely unself-conscious. And I thought, not for the first time and certainly not for the last, that I could spend the rest of my life standing next to this man and it would never feel like anything other than exactly right.

We had lost something. That was true, and it would always be true, and there would be more moments like this one. Moments when the grief showed up uninvited, sat down next to the joy, and refused to leave. I was learning that it was just part of it that you did not get to have the love without also carrying the loss. That they were not opposites. They were just two things that lived cohesively within you.

But I had Joel's hand at my back, Piper crying happy tears on a screen, and a brand-new baby named Auley, who had arrived at 11:57 on St. Patrick's Day. Three minutes before midnight, three minutes before the day that had changed everything for Joel and me. If that was not the universe doing its thing, I did not know what was.

I leaned into Joel's side just slightly.

He dropped a kiss onto the top of my head.

Everett made a gagging sound.

Lola elbowed him hard enough that he actually yelped.

I laughed, and this time it was only one thing. It was just pure and simple happiness.

epilogue

emma

5 MONTHS LATER...

Joel and I had just gotten back from spending a few weeks in Pine Hills. August was one of my favorite times back home because it was warm, but also had an itch to it — that particular restlessness that came when summer knew it was almost over and hadn't quite decided how to feel about it. The trees were still full and green, but the light had shifted, going golden earlier in the evenings, laying itself across the lake in long warm strips that made everything look like a memory even while you were still living inside it.

We had celebrated with pretty much the whole town for a belated wedding party. There was a giant tent and dance floor my parents had put up in their backyard, strung with so many lights it looked like someone had pulled the stars down and arranged them just for us. The music, the cake, the food — everything was beautiful. My mother had cried approximately seven times. My father had given a toast that made even Everett tear up, though he blamed it on the whiskey, and we were all graciously letting him. Joel had danced with me in the middle of that backyard under all those lights, and I had thought, not for the first time and not for the last, how strange and wonderful it was that the boy who had shown up at my pool when I was ten years old was now my husband. That life had been building toward this the whole time, quietly and patiently, even when we were doing everything in our power to get in its way.

Now, as we settled back into the cottage, I stood in the doorway of the sunroom and looked over at Joel in his favorite spot — the wide armchair by the window that faced the sea, the one he had claimed approximately forty-eight hours after moving in and had not relinquished since. He stretched his long legs out, one hand resting on the chair arm, the other holding the book he wasn't quite reading anymore, his eyes soft and unfocused on the middle distance. He looked so peaceful. So content. Like a man who had arrived somewhere he had been trying to get to for a very long time and was finally, fully, letting himself be there.

I leaned against the doorframe and just watched him for a moment.

Joel had moved in immediately after we got married. He had been staying at a hotel a few days before St. Patrick's, so it was a relief he didn't have to find a place — he had simply stopped leaving, which felt exactly right and required almost no discussion at all. We had been planning to live together before I broke up with him, so in a way, we were just picking up a life we had already half-built, dusting it off, and setting it back on its feet.

And it was so easy. That was the thing that still surprised me sometimes, even now. After nine years of hiding and all the hurt that came after, I had braced myself for the adjustment period — for the learning curve of sharing a space and a life with someone, for the friction that was supposed to come with it. But there wasn't much friction. There was just — Joel. Everywhere I looked, woven into everything.

I looked at the walls and saw the art we had chosen together on a rainy Saturday at a gallery in the city, the two of us arguing amiably about whether the large seascape was too on-the-nose for a cottage that already looked directly at the sea. Joel had won that argument. He was right — it was perfect. I looked at the bookshelves and saw his books alongside mine, spines of different heights and colors, his annotations occasionally bleeding through to the edges when he had borrowed one of mine and forgotten himself. I saw the photographs — us at the Pine Hills wedding party, me laughing at something off-camera while Joel watched me with that expression he thought I didn't notice, the one that made my whole chest warm; the two of us on the cliffs in the early weeks of summer when the light was still doing that extraordinary Irish thing; a candid Lola had taken in the kitchen that I had immediately framed because it caught us in the middle of something ordinary and made it look like a painting.

Joel's room had become his office — though he refused to stop calling it Joel's Room, which I found privately delightful and pretended to find annoying. He said it felt like his because of everything I had chosen for it, because every piece of furniture and every object in that room had been picked specifically with him in mind before either of us knew what was coming. He thought that was the most Emma Manning thing he had ever heard in his life. The only thing that had migrated out was the Killarney jewelry casket, which now sat on the dresser in our shared room where every evening Joel emptied his pockets into it — his watch, his keys, his wallet — with the kind of easy domestic ritual that made my heart do something embarrassingly soft every single time I witnessed it.

I loved all of it. I was happy. Not the careful, provisional kind of happiness I had been rationing out to myself in Dublin in the early months — the kind where you're always braced for it to be taken away. This happiness was the other kind. The settled and content kind. The kind that did not announce itself loudly but just sat there, solid and warm, in the background of every ordinary moment.

I loved hearing him sing Creedence Clearwater Revival in the shower every morning — badly, enthusiastically, completely without shame. I loved how he made our coffee, knowing exactly how I took mine without ever having to ask, setting the mug on my side of the kitchen island at the precise moment I came downstairs like he had an internal clock calibrated specifically to me. At night I loved how he always appeared at my desk with a glass of wine without being asked, and then stood behind my chair and worked the tension out of my shoulders with both hands because he had correctly identified that I had spent the entire day hunched over my computer and had decided, entirely on his own, that this was something he could fix.

"You're staring at me," Joel said, without looking up from his book.

"I'm appreciating you," I said. "There's a difference."

He looked up then, the corner of his mouth pulling into that particular half-smile that I had been cataloguing since I was ten years old and still was not entirely immune to.

"Come here." He said.

I crossed the sunroom, and he shifted in the armchair, making room, and I folded myself into the space beside him the way I had been doing for months now — his arm around me, my legs draped over his, the sea going grey and gold outside the window as the afternoon light started to change.

He pressed his lips to my temple and went back to his book.

I looked out at the water.

Everything just fit. Everything felt right. It felt like we were meant to be here. Right here in this cottage, in this life, with the sea outside and Creedence coming from the shower every morning and the Killarney box on the dresser and all of his books mixed up with all of mine on the shelves until you couldn't tell where one of us ended and the other began.

Which, when I thought about it, was exactly how it had always been.

We had just taken the long way to get here.

The very, lengthy way.

But we made it.

And standing in this sunroom with Joel's arm around me and the Irish summer light going golden outside the window, I would not have changed a single step of it.

Not one.

the end

a note from laramie

When I sat down to write Emma and Joel's story, I knew from the very beginning that it was not going to be a simple one. Nine years of a secret, a broken heart, an ocean between them—that was always my plan. But somewhere in the writing, Emma told me something I was not expecting. And when a character tells you something, you listen.

The pregnancy loss and the medical abortion in this story were not decisions I made lightly. I added them because Emma needed something that would crack her open completely. Something that would make leaving feel like the only possible act of love she had left. Everything that followed after the diagnosis of holoprosencephaly, was that thing. It was devastating to write. It was also, I believe, necessary.

Holoprosencephaly is a real condition in which the embryonic brain fails to divide properly. It is rare, it is heartbreaking, and it is one of the many reasons that pregnancy loss takes so many different forms. I wanted to be accurate and respectful in how I portrayed it because real families live this reality, and they deserve to see their experience treated with care. Not just used carelessly as a plot device, but handled with the weight and tenderness it deserves.

The medical abortion discussed, a D&E procedure, which is standard medical care in cases like hers, is also real, and I included it deliberately. Women make this decision in some of the hardest moments of their lives, sometimes alone, sometimes in silence, sometimes while simultaneously trying to protect the people they love from the weight of it. That is Emma's story exactly. I wanted her experience to be visible because so many women carry this in private and never see themselves reflected on the page.

I also wanted to show what happens when grief is carried alone for too long. What it costs. What it takes from you. And what it looks like when someone finally says "*You should have let me grieve with you.*"

I know these are highly sensitive topics. I know not every reader will agree with every choice Emma made or that I as the author made. But I wrote her and this story with full compassion and without judgment, because she and the story deserved that. Because every woman who has been in her position deserves that.

If this story touched something in you, if Emma's grief felt familiar, if you have carried something similar in your own quiet way, please know that you are not alone. Support for pregnancy loss is available, and you deserve to have someone sit with you in it.

Thank you for trusting me with this story. Thank you for reading all the way to the end. Joel and Emma fought hard to get here, and so did I.

With all my love, support, and care,

Laramie

acknowledgments

This book was a lot to write in a short amount of time. But it happened. Yay!

As with every story I write, I want to thank so many people. But with this one, I am going to keep it brief.

Thank you to Marta, my cover designer, for keeping all three books in the Pine Hills Series on brand. Three books in and you have never missed. I greatly appreciate you.

Thank you to Mountain Hops and Cygnet Brewing for giving me quiet space to write in the evenings. Some of the best pages in this book were written with a drink in hand at one of your tables and I am not even a little sorry about it.

Thank you to the Natrona County Library for also being a sanctuary for my words. There is something poetic about writing a book in a library. With libraries and books being under attack, make sure to go support your local library. They need all of the love and endless support because they support all of us in their respective communities.

Thank you to my dear husband for holding down the fort while I disappeared to go write so I wouldn't be endlessly interrupted by our two boys, two dogs, and one cat. You are the real MVP and I owe you approximately one thousand dinners...jk.

Lastly, I know I touched on some very sensitive topics in this story. But I truly felt it was necessary for Emma and Joel to talk about.

about the author

Laramie Cummings is a rising author who refuses to stay boxed into just one genre—her imagination knows no limits! By day, she navigates the fast-paced world of fintech, but off the clock, her life is a delightful juggling act. She's a proud mom to two rambunctious kids, a spirited partner to her husband, and the ringmaster to a quirky pet duo: a dog and a cat who's convinced it's one too. When she's not spinning stories or chasing the next big idea, you might catch her reading, skiing, or creating a coloring book.

also by laramie cummings

Coloring Books

Color Wyoming

Detective Demi: A Coloring Storybook

Pine Hill Series

Second Chance Christmas

Love in the Stacks

www.ingramcontent.com/pod-product-compliance
Lightning Source LLC
LaVergne TN
LVHW091006080826
845145LV00003B/1155

* 9 7 8 1 9 6 7 5 9 4 0 6 1 *